Blonde Ambition

Also by Zoey Dean

THE A-LIST

GIRLS ON FILM

Blonde Ambition

An A-List Novel

by
Zoey Dean

LITTLE, BROWN AND COMPANY
New York ❧ Boston

For Sam, Emma, and Carrie

Little, Brown and Company

Time Warner Book Group
1271 Avenue of the Americas, New York, NY 10020
Visit our Web site at www.lb-teens.com

First Edition

Produced by 17th Street Productions,
an Alloy company
151 West 26th Street, New York, NY 10001

Cover photography (foreground image) copyright Pure/Nonstock
Cover photography (background image) copyright Ken Biggs/Stone

Library of Congress Cataloging-in-Publication Data

Dean, Zoey.
  Blonde ambition / by Zoey Dean.— 1st ed.
      p. cm. — (The A-list ; #3)
  Summary: While Anna's new job as intern on the hottest television show brings her into contact with an interesting new man and helps her see how possessive Ben has become, Cammie sets her sights on Adam.
  ISBN 0-316-73474-8
  I. Title. II. Series: The A-list ; #3.
  [1. Television production and direction—Fiction. 2. Interpersonal relations—Fiction. 3. High schools—Fiction. 4. Schools—Fiction. 5. Los Angeles (Calif.)—Fiction.]
PZ7.D3473Bl 2004
[Fic]--dc22

                                                        2004008638

10 9 8 7 6 5 4 3 2 1

CWO

Printed in the United States of America

"Taking joy in living is a woman's best cosmetic."
—Rosalind Russell

Prologue

Inside suite 15 at the six-hundred-bucks-per-night Montecito Inn in Santa Barbara, California, seventeen-year-old Anna Percy stretched languidly and took in her reflection in the antique mirror over the Van Lutz chest of drawers. Same long blond hair, classic high-cheekboned, patrician features that she'd inherited from her patrician mother. But for the first time in her life she looked, she thought, wild and free.

Those were two adjectives that never came to anyone's mind in describing her, she was certain. Cerebral, yes. Cautious—way too often. But wild? And free? The way her best friend, Cynthia Baltres back in Manhattan, was certainly described on a regular basis? Never.

Yet the deed had finally been done. Ben Birnbaum, the guy who at that very moment was bringing her back a glass of fresh-squeezed orange juice just delivered by room service, had done it.

Only two weeks earlier Anna had left behind her safe, elite life on the Upper East Side of New York to move in with her father in Beverly Hills. She'd hoped, like so many over two centuries of coming to California, to reinvent herself. As she took the juice from Ben, who looked about as hot sans shirt as was possible without actually igniting flammable objects, she smiled.

Mission accomplished.

"Hungry?" Ben asked. He sat next to her and leaned in for a kiss.

"Starved, actually," she admitted, sipping her juice. "You've kept me prisoner in this room for twenty-four hours without food or water."

"Prisoner, huh?" He traced a teasing finger down from her collarbone. "I don't seem to recall any protest."

Beyond true. But Ben's lips made Anna forget about food, and senior year at Beverly Hills High, and all the problems with her screwed-up family. She was able to shut down her constantly thinking/planning/analyzing mind and lose herself to the moment. The world outside suite 15 had ceased to exist. The sixty-dollar post-dinner breakfast they'd ordered remained on the tray. There was nothing in the universe but Ben.

Like a Sister

R *innng.*
Bells kept going off in Anna's head.

Riiing.

Her eyes flicked open. She could just make out the ceiling fan blades swirling the ocean breezes around their moonlit room.

Riing. Now she realized the sound was coming from her cell phone in her purse. She vaguely recalled leaving it on the window seat, whose view overlooked the magnificent beach. Ben was asleep on his back, with one arm flung over his head. His short brown hair was tousled, and she knew how electric blue his eyes were under the closed eyelids. The bulge of his bicep was golden against the white Egyptian cotton, hand-embroidered sheets.

The ringing stopped. Good. The real world could wait for however long she wanted it to wait. She snuggled against Ben. Her phone rang again.

She turned to see the red numerals on the clock radio. Six in the morning. She sat up with a start, heart pounding. Who'd call twice at six in the morning unless it was a disaster? Or a drunk reaching a wrong number? Damn. She threw back the covers and padded across the room, locating her purse and her Motorola cell phone by the fourth ring. She flipped it open. "Hello?"

"Anna?"

Not a drunk. Her father.

"It's Dad. Hey, sorry to wake you, but—"

"What happened?" Anna hissed.

"Good news. About Susan."

Susan? Her sister? He was calling at six in the morning with good news about her sister? Susan hated their father. And with good reason. He'd paid off Susan's college boyfriend to dump her because he and Anna's mother had deemed him "inappropriate." Fifty thousand dollars and the guy was outta there. Anna felt sick again just remembering. So what could be good?

"I'm taking her to rehab. In fact, she insists," her father went on. "So I've kinda got a dilemma here."

"Hold on, Dad." Not wanting to awaken Ben, Anna went into the bathroom and closed the door. "Dad, what's the dilemma? That's great news."

"Yeah, but I'm afraid she's gonna change her mind. And she says she wants to see you before we go. To White Mountains, in Arizona."

"Where is she now?" Anna asked.

"She went back to the Beverly Hills Hotel."

"Don't let her out of your sight," Anna commanded.

Her dad laughed. "Not a chance of that. She's at her

bungalow, packing. I'm in the lobby. And I've got her car keys."

"That's good," Anna allowed.

"So, can you come?" Jonathan asked. "For a breakfast before we take off?"

"Sure, Dad," Anna said automatically, without giving thought to logistics . . . the ungodly hour . . . the gorgeous naked boy lying in her hotel bed . . . the drive . . . the gorgeous naked boy lying in her hotel bed. . . . She was just so pleased that her sister had finally decided to make a positive change in her life.

"Where are you? I'll pick you up," Jonathan offered.

In Santa Barbara, screwing my boyfriend.

Ha! How freeing it would be to actually say something like that. But it was pure fantasy. The reality was that in true good daughter form, she'd be ready to leave in fifteen minutes and would arrive in Beverly Hills within the half hour.

"Oh, that's okay. I'm at my friend Sam's. I can be there in an hour and a half or so. Stay at the hotel. We'll eat in the Polo Lounge."

Fortunately Jonathan Percy wasn't the kind of father who'd give Anna's answer pause. If she said she was at Sam's, that's where she was. No questions asked. Never mind that Sam lived approximately six minutes from the Beverly Hills Hotel.

"Thanks for this, Anna," her father said.

Anna hung up, went back into the bedroom, and shook Ben awake. He was groggy but focused quickly when she explained the problem. "So I've got to go," Anna concluded.

Instead of jumping out of bed immediately to help get their stuff together, Ben wrapped his arms around her. "What's with us, Anna?" he murmured. "We're both trying to fix our fucked-up families. Maybe it's time they took care of themselves."

She gently pulled out of his embrace. "I really have to go, Ben."

His hands dropped to his sides. "I guess I just didn't want this to end."

Neither did she. But she couldn't concentrate on him now. She kissed him quickly—after a fast shower they packed up and departed. Since she'd driven to Santa Barbara alone and Ben had surprised her there, they had two cars and drove back to Los Angeles separately. They convoyed it all the way to the entrance to the Beverly Hills Hotel on Sunset Boulevard, where Ben beeped his horn twice and turned toward his parents' house.

Ten minutes later she was hugging her older sister, Susan, in the Polo Lounge at the world-famous hotel while their father waited discreetly in the lobby.

"I fucking hate myself, you know," Susan said after they'd embraced.

"That's a good reason to go to rehab, I guess," Anna said with a smile.

Susan chuckled and sat down at a table for three. "You should hate me, too." Rather than her usual black-on-black rock-and-roll regalia, she was dressed in a simple pair of jeans and crew neck sweater. "All I do is fuck up your life."

"Isn't that what big sisters are for?" Anna quipped.

"Poor you," Susan muttered.

Anna hadn't been expecting an angry retort. What had she done other than *not* disagree with Susan? Maybe that was the problem. Still, Anna wasn't up for pretending that Susan's behavior was anything short of unacceptable. Instead she glossed over Susan's remark.

"So, what prompted this smart decision?" she asked as a waiter poured her coffee. All around them, on the open-air patio of the Polo Lounge, power breakfasts were in progress. But not the kind of power breakfasts you'd find at the Four Seasons in New York City, where everyone was in suits and ties. Los Angeles was relentlessly informal, and the garb of the Polo Lounge breakfasters reflected that. There were plenty of men in jeans and T-shirts, even tennis clothes. But from the number of scripts open on tables and movie stars who even Anna recognized, it was clear that the Polo Lounge was one of Hollywood's deal-making meccas.

"Turns out the Steinberg debacle wasn't enough excitement for one week. So I went to a club," Susan said self-mockingly—defensively. "I felt like dancing, you know? Don't you ever just feel like dancing? This chick I knew from Trinity School goes to USC now. We arranged to meet. But the bitch never showed. I got polluted. Really polluted. A bouncer drove me home— Arman or Eman or something. I think."

"You're lucky nothing worse happened." Anna knew she was being blunt but figured that a little fear never hurt anyone.

"I know. That's why I've had enough. The end."

"You think you can stick with it this time?"

Susan shrugged. "I hope so."

Just then Anna heard someone creep up from behind her.

"May I join you two?"

The two girls looked up. There stood their father, Jonathan Percy. Tall, lean, and tan, he was an investment banker with a very un-investment-banker spiky haircut and movie-star blue eyes. Susan waved him to the open chair at their table, and Jonathan sat down.

"It's good that you're driving her, Dad," Anna said. "Really."

Jonathan's eyes slid to Susan's. "If she doesn't kill me before I get her there."

Susan held her palms up. "No weapons on me, Dad."

He attempted a half smile and turned to Anna. "Django should be along any minute. He'll get Susan's car back to the agency and bring you home. I should be back in a couple of days at the latest."

Django Simms was Jonathan's driver. Cute, young, a jazz musician, and a man of mystery, Django and Anna had hit it off right away. He lived in the guesthouse on the Percy property in Beverly Hills.

"I'll be fine. And—"

"Anna?"

She looked up.

Ben was standing at the side of their table. The same Ben who'd beeped his farewell at her a few minutes ago on Sunset Boulevard. The same Ben with whom she'd spent the previous day and night in several compromising positions.

"Ben," Anna said. Which was certainly stating the obvious, but she was just so shocked to see him.

"I wanted to make sure everything was okay," he explained. Before Anna could muster a response to that, Ben held out a hand to her father. "Hi, I'm Ben Birnbaum."

Jonathan stood and shook it. "Jonathan Percy. Anna's mentioned you."

Anna noticed the ice in her father's voice. She couldn't really blame him. Last he'd heard, Ben had broken Anna's heart.

"Everything's okay, Dad," Anna murmured, since her father was still in a killer eye lock with Ben. "Would you like to join us?" she asked Ben, at the same time willing him to spurn her always-gracious-under-pressure offer.

"Sure, thanks."

Ben pulled up a chair from the next table, then took Anna's hand. As much as Anna liked him, she felt like snatching it back. What was he doing here, for God's sake?

"Ben, Ben, Ben," Susan cooed. "I didn't recognize you with your clothes on."

Right. The sauna at V's spa, Anna realized. Her sister had met Ben in the sauna not more than seventy-two hours before. But he'd had his clothes on. Well, not his shirt, maybe, but—

"Nice to see you again, too," Ben said, leaning closer to Susan. "How are you feeling, really?"

"Super-duper," Susan sang out with a too-bright smile.

Anna gave Ben a significant look that meant: *Please realize you've made an error in judgment, excuse yourself, and go.* But evidently their brains weren't communicating, because all he did was squeeze the hand that he still held tightly.

Jonathan ignored Ben and checked his Rolex. "We really should get going, Susan."

"Right," Susan agreed. "Well, Ben, nice of you to pop in like this on our *intimate family breakfast.*"

"I wanted to be here," Ben answered in earnest. Anna couldn't tell if he was glossing over Susan's dig or if he was oblivious to it entirely.

"I hate goodbyes," she told Anna, "so let's skip it. I'm off like a dirty shirt."

Anna stood, too, as did her father and Ben. "No goodbyes," she promised her sister as a lump formed in her throat. "But . . . good luck."

"Oh, fuck it. C'mere." Susan pulled Anna close and hugged her hard. "Love you like a sister, sister. You ready to go, Dad?"

Jonathan Percy nodded, took a hundred-dollar bill out of his wallet, and left it on the table. "For breakfast," he told Anna, then shot Ben a last warning look. "I'll call you from the road," he added to his daughter.

"Hang in there, Susan," Ben called. "We're rooting for you."

"We're rooting for you"? But Anna didn't have time to dwell on Ben's inappropriate words.

Anna watched as her father put his arm around Susan's shoulders and ushered her out of the Polo Lounge and toward the lobby.

Ben squeezed Anna's arm. "You okay?" he asked.

"I'm fine. But . . . I think I'll just go home and . . . take a nap," Anna said.

Now he slid both hands around her waist. "Dad's gone," he pointed out. "We could nap together."

But after Ben's out-of-nowhere arrival, she really didn't feel like inviting him under her covers. "Another time," she promised.

The valets brought their cars around to the front of the hotel. Ben followed Anna out to Sunset Boulevard, then once again they sped off in different directions. But Anna kept checking her rearview mirror until she turned into her father's circular driveway, half expecting to see that Ben had followed her home.

Brownie Points for the Pedigree

Six hours after Susan and her father departed for Arizona, Anna stood by the floor-to-ceiling glass wall of the Apex Talent Agency large conference room and looked west, out toward Santa Monica and then the Pacific. It was one of those golden California afternoons with a cerulean blue sky and only a few puffy cumulus clouds on the horizon. A strong west wind was blowing—Anna could hear the soft moan as a gust whooshed past the sides of the Apex building. But the westerly breeze had also scrubbed the ever-present air pollution from the Los Angeles basin and pushed it east. Fifty miles away, in the San Bernadino Valley, where a working couple with regular jobs might actually afford a house, people were choking on the smoggy airborne fruits of the Los Angeles freeways. Meanwhile Anna's view to the horizon was crystalline.

Which, Anna realized, was somehow quintessentially L.A.

She took out her cell phone, knowing that she still needed to talk to Adam Flood—to tell him that she was back with Ben. She dialed Adam's number. But again there was no answer. She left a message saying that she'd call him later.

"Anna? Might I have a word? I don't have much time."

Anna put away her phone as Margaret Cunningham strode into the conference room. One of three lead partners in Apex, she was the person who had offered Anna the internship in the first place. She was also her father's current girlfriend. In a city where a forty-five-year-old, once-divorced man with a twenty-one-year-old girlfriend was the norm, the relationship was an aberration. Margaret was at least the same age as Jonathan Percy. The bizarre thing was, Margaret bore a more-than-passing resemblance to Anna's mother, Jane Percy. The same blunt-cut blond hair, the patrician features, the understated makeup, the preference for Armani suits and vintage Chanel—even the well-bred East Coast WASP diction.

Anna could feel her heartbeat speed up as she slid into one of the leather chairs at the conference table; she faced the door. Margaret took a seat at the head of the table. Having been dressed down by her own mother many a time, Anna was not looking forward to being reprimanded by Margaret.

"I just got off the phone with your father," Margaret said. "I'm very happy to hear that your sister has decided to return to rehabilitation. White Mountains has a very fine reputation."

"I'm glad, too." Anna's first reaction was relief. She'd felt certain that Margaret would simply send her packing because of what had happened at the party, but perhaps she was separating Anna from her sister and her sister's problems. Now, that would be refreshing. Not to mention fair.

It was ironic, really. An internship at a talent agency wasn't something she'd ever wanted. Anna's heart was in the literary world. But now Anna found herself excited about being a part of it, open to the new experiences it might bring. That was the reason, she kept reminding herself, she'd moved west in the first place.

And now here she was, about to lose her internship right after it began, all because Susan had shown up at an industry party completely drunk and had made a scene. Anna and Sam had rescued Susan. If Anna had to do it all over again, she'd do exactly the same thing. It wouldn't be the first time Anna had suffered for Susan's mistakes.

Margaret folded her hands and continued. "Also, I'm pleasantly surprised that your father has decided to stay in Arizona for a few days. He says it's to make sure that Susan doesn't check herself out, but I suspect it's really so he can drive up and see the Grand Canyon."

Anna nodded. Her father had sent her a long e-mail from his laptop—she was totally up to speed on everything that Margaret was telling her.

"Are you doing okay at home? By yourself?"

"Sure. In New York, I was alone a lot. My mother is

on a lot of committees and—" Anna stopped herself.
There was no reason to bring up her mother right
now—Anna was sure that Margaret had heard all about
her mother. "I'm used to taking care of myself. I'm
fine."

"Well, if you need anything, your father asked me to
help. So call me."

"Thank you, that's very kind of you." As Anna
spoke, a sunbeam cut through the window and against
the far wall, as if the ray of hope had actually come to
life. She couldn't believe it. Margaret was actually
befriending her. Her heart rate slowed to something
approaching normal.

"So," Margaret asked. "Shall we discuss the events of
this past weekend? At the Steinbergs' party?"

Anna had already mentally rehearsed for this
moment. "I would like to say that I am sorry I didn't
stick closer to Brock Franklin. He's an Apex client; you
asked me to attend the party with him on Apex's
behalf, and I should have handled that in a more professional manner. I apologize."

"And?" Margaret prompted.

Anna sat silent. She had been well raised on the subject of airing family laundry in public: it just wasn't done.

Margaret seemed to suck in her cheeks a bit, making
her sharp cheekbones stand out. "There is the matter of
your sister and her snap decision to test the water
purity of the Feinbergs' backyard fountain. With her
mouth and in her underwear."

Anna kept her voice steady. "My sister has a substance abuse problem. We've already addressed that. I wish I could have prevented her behavior. But I can't. That's a lesson that's hard to accept."

"She made her problem abundantly clear to every guest at the party."

Anna opened her mouth to speak, but Margaret held up a restraining finger. "I don't hold you responsible for that problem, Anna. I do hold you responsible for the way you handled it. Running to your sister's aid and then departing with her was completely unacceptable. Not to mention out of line. Not to mention an embarrassment to this agency. And to me personally."

Anna could feel her face redden. It didn't happen very often. But it was equally rare for her to sit through such a dressing-down by an authority figure.

"I'm sorry for that." Anna tried to make her apology sound as heartfelt as it was.

"I should hope so. It was a black eye for the agency."

Anna cocked her head. She'd already apologized from the bottom of her heart. What else did Margaret want her to do? "With all due respect, Margaret, I think there's some blame to be shared here. You knew about my sister's problems. Why would you have wanted her to be at a party like that when she'd only half completed her rehab? If you're going to fire me, just fire me. I can handle it."

Margaret tapped a pencil on the table. "Perhaps you've led a privileged life for so long that you don't know what it means to be in a subordinate position. That is most unfortunate, Anna. I asked you here assuming you were willing to listen. What I'm telling you isn't my position alone, but the position of the agency. I spoke about this with my associates, and this is a group decision."

Anna stood and walked to the door, fully prepared to depart with grace and dignity. "Fine. I understand that. You speak for Apex. Apex invited Susan to that party because she went to school with Apex's client, Brock Franklin. You did that because you thought it might benefit you. You never gave a thought to how it might affect Susan. Asking her to be there was irresponsible. Far more irresponsible than I might have been with Brock."

Margaret sighed. "Are you finished?"

"No," Anna said. She knew this wasn't going to be the last time she'd see Margaret. It was more important for Margaret to know what kind of person she was than for her to work as an intern at the agency. "I'm grateful that you gave me this chance at Apex. I really am. But Susan is my sister. If Susan had been your sister, I hope you would have done exactly what I did."

From behind Anna came the sound of one person clapping. Anna whirled, shocked to see Clark Sheppard, Cammie's father, another of the Apex agency partners, staring at her with raised eyebrows.

"Who are you?" he asked.

"Anna Percy. For about ten minutes I was an intern here."

"You still are," Clark said bluntly.

"Clark," Margaret cut in, not raising her voice one iota. "We talked about this, remember? I'm going to be the one to decide whether she goes or stays."

"Anna, wait outside." Clark pointed toward the hallway outside the conference room. "We'll be with you momentarily."

Anna exited. She could see Clark and Margaret arguing through the glass wall but couldn't hear a word.

It must have been nerves that made her think about clothes. Margaret and Clark were both impeccably turned out. She wore a pantsuit—Anna guessed it was Ralph Lauren—and his suit was obviously custom-made. Sam had explained the bizarre show business clothing pecking order to her: Writers dressed like bums. Producers dressed like writers, except they wore baseball caps to cover their hair loss. Directors dressed like producers, except that they were frequently tanned from being outside while on location. Actors dressed like bums but looked better since they spent their free time in the gym if they were earning a living or running in the park if they weren't. If they were going to be photographed, they wore designer clothes and jewels provided gratis because the designers wanted the free publicity. In fact, the only people who dressed like New York businesspeople were agents.

Clark clearly didn't share Margaret's understated style. Though Anna couldn't hear what he was saying, she could see him in there, waving his arms around. At one point a finger stabbed the air in Margaret's direction. Then he swung the door open and beckoned Anna back inside.

"You're not working with Margaret anymore," he barked.

"I'm already well aware of that fact," Anna replied.

"You're still an intern, though," Clark added.

Anna was confused. "I don't know that I—"

"You don't have to know; you're an intern, for chrissake, so just listen. You are not to talk to Margaret Cunningham. That means if you pass her in the hall or see her in the bathroom, you are not even to look at her. *She's dead to you.* Understand?"

Anna thought about explaining that it would be a bit difficult for Margaret to be dead to her since there was a reasonable chance on any given morning that she'd encounter Margaret at her breakfast table, drinking her father's coffee. Then she thought better of it. Then she thought about declining this offer—whatever it was. She couldn't imagine why Mr. Sheppard had intervened on her behalf.

The old Anna Percy would have certainly declined. She could only imagine what her mother would think of crass Clark Sheppard: he might wear a three-thousand-dollar suit, but that didn't change the lack of class of the man inside it.

Screw it, Anna thought.

"Yes sir," she said brightly. She snuck a final look at Margaret. Her demeanor hadn't changed, but her eyes were flecked with rage—not at Anna, but at Clark. Clearly she had been out-manipulated by Cammie's father in some arcane game of intra-office politics.

"See me in my office in ten minutes, Anna. It's the biggest one, on the corner. This meeting is over."

When Anna approached the corner that held Clark's office, his assistant, Gerard, told her it was okay to enter the inner sanctum. Gerard was in his twenties, an obvious athlete with extremely broad shoulders. He wore a white shirt and red tie.

Anna opened the door. Clark was in a huge black chair behind his desk—a sleek metal-and-glass number—gabbing away into his telephone headpiece. On the tabletop were two multiple-extension telephones plus a flat-screen computer monitor and a keyboard. One entire wall of the office was lined with television sets, DVD players, and audio equipment as well as a stack of scripts that went from floor to ceiling. He motioned for Anna to come in and sit down. She did, taking a seat on the lowest couch in the history of low, buttery leather couches. Behind Clark and to her left were more of those floor-to-ceiling wall windows.

"Well, I don't give a good goddamn what *Quentin* thinks or how much *Quentin* believes that my client would want to work with him," Clark bellowed into the tiny microphone. "Her quote is fifteen mil, it's always fifteen mil, it's always gonna be fifteen mil, but if you piss me off any more, it's gonna be twenty mil. If *Quentin* can't get your goddamn studio to write a check for fifteen mil, he can call Madonna. I hear she's always available!"

He slammed down the phone and then smiled up at Anna. "Studios," he said lightly. "The guys in business affairs are all masochists. Otherwise they'd quit after their first conversation with me. So, tell me about you, Anna Percy." His eyes went to his Rolex. "Fast."

Anna gave Clark the quick version of her life—her recent move from Manhattan to Beverly Hills, that she was attending high school here, and that her father and Margaret were seeing each other. She figured that if she didn't tell him, he'd find out anyway, so better for him to hear it from her.

"Where'd you go to school in Manhattan?"

"Trinity."

"Where do you go here?"

"Beverly Hills High School."

Clark smiled thinly. "You know my daughter?" He turned around a photograph of Cammie that was at least three years old.

Details would be counterproductive. Anna merely said, "Yes."

"You friends?"

"We know some of the same people, I think," Anna said carefully.

"Cammie wants your gig tomorrow, it's hers. But she doesn't want it. She never wanted it, and she'll never want it. No interest in the business. So, Anna Percy, you watch a lot of TV?"

"No."

"Good answer. Which means you've never heard of *Hermosa Beach*. Teen-oriented soap kinda thing. *Beverly Hills 90210* on a beach meets *Upstairs, Downstairs*. Rich kids and the poor help, that kinda thing. You know those shows?"

Anna shook her head. Clark just reached for a script on his desk and handed it to Anna. There was a noise in the doorway. Anna looked up.

There stood Cammie Sheppard, looking as gorgeous as Cammie always looked but also, at the moment, more than shocked to find Anna in her father's office. "Hi, Anna," she said smoothly. "How nice to see you."

Which, Anna knew, actually translated to: *Die, bitch.*

But Anna smiled politely anyway.

Clark went to the door, took his daughter by the arm, and apparently spoke to her outside. Then Clark returned and closed the door behind him. "Where was I?"

"*Hermosa Beach*," Anna reminded.

"Right." Clark paced as he spoke. "Anyway, the show just started shooting. Our agency is as involved in the production as the network that will air it. It premieres in two weeks, and don't listen to the good buzz on the street, because right now it's in deep shit. Studio and network can't agree on what to do. Assholes. All of 'em. So you're gonna spend a lot of time on *H. B.* Got it?"

Anna's head was swimming. "I do have one question, Mr. Sheppard."

"Shoot."

"Why me? There have got to be a thousand people in this city more qualified to work with you on this."

"Any kid who can stand toe to toe with Margaret Cunningham has *cojones*. I like *cojones*. You never raised your voice, but you held your own. Plus you get brownie points for the pedigree. Your looks don't hurt, either."

Anna couldn't quite decide if this was a compliment or an insult.

"What about what Margaret said in there?" Anna wondered aloud. "She said that me being fired was a group decision."

"It was," Clark said. "Then I changed my mind. So you remember what I said about Margaret. She's dead to you. You fuck up, you're out. Leave your address with my assistant, and I'll send over the show bible. Clear your weekend. We're going to be busy." Anna could see his foot tapping the floor under his desk, a clear sign that he was ready for her to leave his office.

She stood—the couch so low that getting to one's feet was more easily said than done—shook Clark's hand, and said she was looking forward to working with him. By the time she left the office, he was already barking commands to Gerard.

Anna looked both ways when she got outside his door, thoroughly prepared for a confrontation with Cammie. Fortunately she wasn't around.

"Anna!" Margaret headed in her direction. "Anna, can you stop in my office before you go?"

She's dead to you. Clark's words came back to her.

Maybe she'd call Margaret from home to let her know that she really didn't have any hard feelings. But right now Anna knew that Clark Sheppard might be watching her. So as she passed Margaret, she kept her eyes fixed on the carpet.

Welcome to Hollywood.

Minor Players

Table 8 on Melrose Avenue was the hottest new restaurant in Los Angeles. Upstairs was a tattoo parlor, where local hipsters and daring girls from Lakewood came to get painted and pierced. Downstairs from the parlor was Table 8, the "it" place of the moment, where it was impossible for anyone—tattooed or tattoo-free—to get a reservation.

But Samantha Sharpe wasn't anyone. She was the daughter of the best-loved movie star in the world, Jackson Sharpe. Her name, associated with a place or a product and read in the supermarket tabloids by the unwashed masses, guaranteed popularity.

At four in the afternoon she'd had her father's assistant, Kiki, call Table 8 to say that Sam Sharpe wanted to book a table for two that evening, in the back. At two minutes after four Sam had her reservation.

The owners of Table 8 were no dummies. They knew that by March, their restaurant would be toast with insiders who'd already moved on to the Next Big Thing. They'd need tourists and diners from Van Nuys and Encino to survive. Giving Sam Sharpe a table today ensured that there would be customers tomorrow.

It seemed to Sam that trying to pick up Adam Flood on the rebound from Anna Percy was the right thing to do. After all, Anna and Adam had met at her own father's wedding when Anna had shown up on Ben's arm as his mystery date. So, actually, Sam was responsible for their having met in the first place. The least she could do was take Adam out for a nice dinner and try and seduce him.

As for Anna being back with Ben, Sam knew it was true because Ben had called her to tell her so. That day at school she and her friends Cammie Sheppard and Dee Young had gone to their favorite place at Westside Pavilion for sushi (although Beverly Hills High hired cooks straight out of the California Culinary Academy, there was just something so *ick* about eating in your high-school cafeteria). When Ben had telephoned, Sam didn't let on to Cammie and Dee who she was talking with. Since they'd simultaneously been on their own cells, they hadn't asked.

Ben couched the call as a thank-you, since Sam was the one who'd told him that Anna had escaped to the Montecito Inn in Santa Barbara. Ben had followed Anna there. Crashing waves, passionate kisses, fade to black.

A hot guy Sam recognized from an underwear billboard walked by her table on his way to the men's room. She immediately sucked in her stomach and tossed her hundred-dollar blowout—plus two thousand dollars' worth of hair extensions—saucily off her shoulders. She was wearing a new Plein Sud electric blue silk shirt with Fini black pants and her favorite black patent leather, stiletto-heeled Jimmy Choo boots. Her makeup was, as always, perfect. But Sam knew that in spite of the thousands she spent on upkeep and maintenance, she was a long way from a ten on the Beverly Hills Hot-or-Not scale. She'd gotten her too-wide nose done, and there was an implant in her naturally receding chin. But there was nothing she could do about her fire-hydrant calves and fat ankles. Sam wasn't even a nine. You couldn't be a nine if your pants size was eight.

The hot guy looked right through Sam. Shit. She decided he was gay and sipped her spring water with mint just for something to do.

Adam was late. While she waited, she felt ambivalent about recent developments. A few days ago she'd thought she wanted Anna. Now that Adam was available, she thought she might want him. Her famous psychiatrist, Dr. Fred, had suggested that Sam was confusing the intimacy of true friendship with the intimacy of sexual love. Sam had no idea. Though she'd had many friends and more than her share of sex, she hadn't had the intimacy part. Ever. With anyone. Maybe she was just acting on the possibility that Adam or Anna was capable of offering this.

"Hey, Sam. Sorry I'm late." Adam kissed her cheek before sliding into his seat.

Sam smiled. There was something so appealing

about Adam. He'd moved with his family to Beverly Hills from Michigan and was probably the most decent guy on the West Coast. That he was offbeat-Ben-Stiller-but-taller, cute, and charming kept him in the margins of the BHH A-list, extra points added because he didn't care about being on it.

"Not a problem," Sam said easily, though normally it irritated the hell out of her not to be the one keeping the other person waiting.

Adam looked around the restaurant. "I told my mom you'd invited me to dinner here. She was duly impressed." He grinned his disarming grin. "And I'm kinda surprised. What's the occasion?"

Before Sam could respond to that, the black-clad waiter was at their table, handing them menus. The name of the restaurant came from the fact that there were only eight appetizers and eight main dishes from which to choose, so the menu fit comfortably into one hand. The waiter, who reeked of cute-struggling-actor, rhapsodized about the various dishes until Sam broke in.

"Tell you what. Bring us half a plate of one of each." She took Adam's menu and handed them both to the waiter.

The waiter faltered a moment. "You want *everything?*"

It was a trick she'd learned from her father. If you ordered everything, you could taste-test each dish and never had to envy what the other person ordered and wish you had ordered it yourself. Of course, half the time Jackson Sharpe ended up not even touching half the dishes since—like his daughter—he was constantly on a diet.

"Everything, thanks," Sam said, which translated to: *Go away. Now.*

Adam winced. "I hope we're planning on taking the leftovers to a homeless shelter or something."

"How about we just mail a donation and call it a day?" Sam suggested. She reached across the table and put her hand atop Adam's. "So, what do you think about Anna?"

Adam shrugged and took a sip of water. "She's her own person. She has to follow her own heart."

"That's incredibly mature," Sam said. "You're not a bit jealous that she spent the last two nights with Ben Birnbaum—"

"What? *Since when?*"

Adam sputtered water, and Sam's hand flew to her mouth. She realized that her assumption about Anna had been wrong—that Anna hadn't spoken to Adam yet.

"Didn't Anna call you?" Sam asked.

"Like, three times today," Adam said. "But I wasn't near the phone. Voice mail picked up. I know she wants to talk to me. She said she was out of town but now she's back."

Sam backpedaled. She suspected that Anna wouldn't be pleased if she learned that Sam had spilled her beans. "Well, it doesn't seem right to be the one to tell—"

Adam looked steadily at Sam. "Come on. I'm a big boy. Tell me."

She told him. Ben and Anna. Anna and Ben. Together. Big time.

Emotions skittered across Adam's face. He rubbed the small star tattoo behind his ear. His shoulders slumped. "I just don't. . . ." He reached for a fresh-baked roll, then put it down again. "I guess I won't understand until I talk to her. Man, love sucks."

"Hey, I have an idea," Sam said, sensing that if she was planning to make a big move on Adam, this wasn't the time. "What are you doing this weekend?"

"Walking my dog and licking my wounds, most likely."

"My dad's doing a cameo in a TV series, *Hermosa Beach*, this weekend, a favor for a friend. It's new this season. There's an after party. Why don't you come with me?"

"I don't think I'll be up for it, Sam. But thanks."

"Oh, come on. Why should you stop having fun just because Anna and Ben are having lots of it?"

Adam grimaced. "Way to rub salt in the ol' wounds."

She touched his hand again. "It'll take your mind off her. I'd really like you to come."

Before Adam could answer, a line of waiters came to the table, carrying their eight first courses: everything from green beans and figs with sliced summer truffles to grilled sweetbreads thinly wrapped in pancetta. Sam looked at the food. None of it appealed to her. Maybe the realization that Adam was nowhere near ready to be thinking of anyone other than Anna Percy had dulled her appetite.

She touched the sleeve of the last waiter.

"On second thought, could you just ask the chef to make me a burger? Medium rare, a slice of tomato, a scooped-out baguette instead of a bun. That'd be great."

The waiter nodded. "Absolutely, Ms. Sharpe. That'll be about ten minutes."

"Hey, aren't you the one who did the Fox show? And was in that video? You are so hot, no lie."

Cammie barely turned her head toward the guy who had just crept up next to her at the bar. It was so dark that she could barely make out his features. But whatever they were, he was short—no more than an inch or two taller than she was. Cammie Sheppard could afford to be choosy. She didn't do short. Besides, he was confusing her with Paris Hilton. And that really *was* an insult, and not just because Cammie had the best implants that money could buy.

That Cammie was an eleven on a looks scale of one to ten was something she took for granted. Her strawberry blond mane and bee-stung lips pretty much guaranteed a plethora of male attention. When you added that to her size-two figure, topped off by perfectly perky D-cup breasts, men were simply going to fall at her feet. It was a given. It wasn't even all that interesting anymore.

At the moment, she was wearing a white velvet Jenny Packham bodysuit with a thong bottom and her lowest Posh jeans, which meant that there was a good six inches of golden, tanned flesh exposed on both sides, all the way to her hip bones. Her hair was in its trademark wild style, and you could ski down her pink Stila lip gloss.

Just because a girl suffered from Beverly Hills ennui didn't mean she should let herself go.

Wordlessly she turned her back and iced the guy out, deeming him unworthy of the energy of a put-down. In fact, Cammie was already wondering why she'd agreed to meet Sam at this new place in Los Feliz near the ABC studios. So what if a variety of flavor-of-the-week under-thirty stars owned it? It was a pain in the ass to get here. As far as Cammie could tell, it was just as boring as every other bar.

"What'd I miss?" Dee Young asked breathlessly, hopping back up on her bar stool. Dee had been in the ladies' room all of five minutes, but from her tone you'd think she'd been in the loo snorting coke for a half hour during a really good movie.

"I found God, Dee," Cammie replied. "I'm taking a vow of chastity."

Dee's round baby blue eyes got even larger. "You mean it just, like, came over you?"

"Joking." Cammie knew better than to joke with Dee. She was the most literal person Cammie had ever known.

With her diminutive size and baby face, Dee appeared to be an innocent. But what Dee lacked in IQ, she more than made up for in raunch. Or at least she had in the past. But Dee had made a recent change, which was why she was sipping iced green tea. Alcohol had not touched her lips in forty-eight hours, she'd restarted her colonics at Zen Nation to purge toxins from her body, and she had recently intensified her class schedule at the Kabbalah Center.

From Cammie's point of view, all this was unbelievably boring since she was sure it wouldn't last. With Dee, nothing ever did. "Where'd you lose Sam?"

"Some girl in the bathroom had a small part in her dad's last film," Dee reported. "They're talking."

This news depressed Cammie even further—more evidence that Sam was changing, too. Sam had never been known for being friendly to minor players from her father's movies, though they always tried to suck up to her. But since she had started spending less time with Cammie and Dee and more with Anna Percy, her behavior had begun to shift.

Anna Percy. That bitch.

In the few weeks that Anna had been in Beverly Hills, she'd proved herself to be the kiss of death. Everything she touched turned to shit for Cammie. It was bad enough that Ben Birnbaum had dropped Cammie—the first guy who ever had—and then fallen hard for East Coast snot Anna. When that relationship fizzled almost before it began, Cammie was delighted. But now Sam was reporting that Ben and Anna were a couple again and Ben was claiming to be in love for the first time!

Which means he never loved me, Cammie thought, a catch in her throat.

Fucking Anna.

"God, this place sucks," Sam said, edging her way over to them through the thick crowd. "Every two-bit wannabe west of the Mississippi is glomming onto me."

Cammie sighed with relief. Now *that* sounded more like the old Sam. Cammie raised one French-manicured finger and signaled the bartender for another round of drinks. He'd pretended to check their IDs, and of course they each had fake passports complete with stamps from Barbados and Antigua. But they could have flashed passes to Knott's Berry Farm for all the scrutiny he gave them.

"Now, about the A-word," Cammie sneered when she had a new drink in front of her. "First of all, I predict that this round of her and Ben will be history within days. Second of all, I happen to know she got fired today from her internship at Apex."

Cammie wasn't certain that Anna had been fired but figured saying so was worth a shot. Her father was notorious for being one of the biggest son-of-a-bitch agents in a town where the title was bestowed with respect. The scene Anna and her sister had caused at the Feinberg party didn't exactly bode well for Anna's future. That Cammie had been with Susan when she got drunk didn't make Cammie feel guilty. Sure, maybe she'd offered Susan a drink. And sure, maybe she'd worked on Susan's insecurities so that Susan would want to drink. So what?

Cammie didn't like Sam's facial reaction to this news, though. "Do not look at me in that tone of voice," Cammie decreed, deliberately mixing the verbs. "It's not my fault if her sister is a lush."

"You were with her when she was polluting her body," Dee pointed out.

Cammie pushed strawberry curls off her face. "The two of you are getting truly boring." She took a long pull on her drink. It was all just so depressing. The only thing that would cheer her up would be a really major shopping spree. No. Ben breaking up with Anna *and* a really major shopping spree.

But a niggling voice in her head reminded her that even if Ben and Anna did break up, he wasn't going to come running back to Cammie's arms.

Hang in There, Cowboy

C ammie stumbled a little on the stone path that led from the circular driveway up to the front door. The mansion they'd moved to after her father married Patrice Koose, also known as the Stepmother from Hell, wasn't as massive as the Sharpe compound. But it was still six thousand luxurious square feet, assessed at well north of four million dollars.

For that kind of money you'd think they could keep up the walkway, Cammie thought as she wedged her key into the front door and punched the code into the security system.

"Ah, Dorothy's back."

The nasty sneer came from the sunken living room. Shit. Her stepmother was up. On top of spending her evening fighting off assholes and hearing about Anna and Ben's love life, she was going to have to deal with the Wicked Witch of the West.

"Up late sticking pins in voodoo dolls, Patrice?" Cammie asked, slipping out of the strappy pink Christian Louboutin heels that were killing her feet.

Patrice sipped something from a bone china cup. She wore a red velvet robe and had her feet propped up on the slate Spanish coffee table that had arrived from Barcelona in time for Christmas. "I thought perhaps we could share a civil five minutes of conversation."

"Doubtful." Cammie picked up her shoes and pushed her hair out of her eyes. "I'm going to bed."

"Oh, that's right. Tomorrow is a school day. I know how concerned you are about your studies."

Cammie frowned at her. "You know, Patrice, you might want to call Dr. Birnbaum tomorrow. Your Botox is wearing off." She padded toward the circular stairs.

"And your stepsister is moving in," Patrice announced loudly.

Cammie turned the words over in her mind. "I don't have a stepsister."

"She's my daughter and I married your father, which makes the two of you . . . whatever." Patrice raised an elegantly dismissive hand. "Anyway, she's moving in. Tomorrow."

"Since when do you have a daughter?"

"Since I gave birth to her fourteen years ago."

Cammie shook her head. This made zero sense. Patrice was a former star and former has-been star whose career had been resurrected by Clark Sheppard. Cammie had read all Patrice's press. There'd been no mention of a daughter.

"Her name is Mia," Patrice went on. "When I had her, I wasn't equipped to raise a daughter and maintain a career. So she's lived with my sister in Valley Village most of her life."

"She's *what?*"

"I'm not going to discuss this with you, Camilla. It's personal business. Suffice to say that I've invited her to move in with us. She and my sister have had some problems of late."

"I don't think so."

"It's up to your father and me. And we've decided. I stayed up to tell you personally. Good night."

"Hold on, Mommy dearest," Cammie insisted, blocking Patrice's path. "There's no way that my father agreed to have your evil spawn move into our house. You hate children. How could you possibly have one?"

But Patrice swept right by her and climbed the stairs, leaving Cammie, her blistered feet, and the six-hundred-dollar sandals that got them that way in her wake.

Wrestling with calculus is not my idea of a good time, Anna thought, tapping her pencil against the black slate rolltop desk in what was now her bedroom. She'd already been accepted to Yale early decision and felt like high school was a thing of the past. But she did have to finish her senior year. And it wasn't in her nature to slack off at much of anything, really.

But things at Beverly Hills High were just so complicated. Or, more specifically, the Adam Flood thing was just so complicated. She *still* hadn't told him about

Ben, but not for lack of trying. She just hadn't been able to reach him by phone.

Guess now's as good a time as any, she thought as she reached for her phone and pressed his number on speed dial.

This time there was no voice mail. "Hello?"

"Adam? It's me, Anna. I need to talk to you."

"I know you've been trying to reach me. But you really don't have to anymore," said Adam. "I know everything."

"But how?"

"Sam. By accident, really. Don't be mad at her. She thought you'd already told me."

Anna swallowed hard, feeling distinctly uncomfortable. "Okay. Maybe . . . we can have lunch tomorrow? To . . . talk?"

Silence.

"Are you there, Adam?"

"I'm here. Everything in the world tells me to say no, but okay. Where?"

"How about . . . Jerry's Deli? Near the Beverly Center?"

"Twelve thirty. See you there."

The phone clicked off. As Anna powered it down, she realized that there was music coming from downstairs. Classical music. But she hadn't left the CD player or radio on. And she doubted that Juanita or Consuela or any of the other half-dozen maids and cooks and bottle washers who looked after her father's every need would have a sudden urge for a Chopin étude.

She tied the belt of her white Ralph Lauren silk robe tighter and padded downstairs, not terribly nervous—there was a superb security system in her father's home. Besides, who was going to tarry for a little classical interlude before they robbed the place?

The instant she got to the bottom of the massive oak staircase, the mystery was solved. There at the Steinway grand, back to her, was Django. Which made sense—Django lived in the guesthouse, had keys to the place, and knew all the security codes. Now Anna remembered that Django had given her a demo tape of his, a jazz piano demo. And hadn't she seen a photograph of Django as a boy, standing in front of a full symphony orchestra?

Not wanting to disturb him, Anna sat at the base of the stairs and listened as Django's fingers danced over the keyboard, the music swirling through the empty house. She kept listening, right through the magnificent silence that followed the last note of the piece. Then she applauded.

Django turned around, grinning. "Well, if it isn't Miss Anna," he drawled, his Louisiana roots evident in his voice.

She stopped and went to him. "You really have to stop calling me that. It sounds like something from *Gone with the Wind.*"

"Anyway, it's fun pissin' you off. You're just such a *lady* about it."

She had to laugh. "The Chopin was beautiful."

"Haven't played it since I was fourteen."

"Why not?"

"It's a long, not very interesting story." Django swung his legs around and regarded Anna in a way that made her suddenly conscious that she had on nothing under her robe but a pale pink La Perla chemise.

Anna resisted the urge to tighten her belt. "Did you know I was upstairs in bed?" She blushed. The words had come out more flirtatiously than she'd intended.

"Kinda," Django acknowledged. "Your car's here. In this town that's a pretty big clue. Anyway, I'm sorry. I should've called first. But I love this piano, and when your dad's around, he doesn't like it to be played."

"It's okay," Anna told him. "I was wrestling with some calculus and losing."

He tipped a nonexistent hat. "Happy to please, ma'am." His eyes flitted over her robe. "So . . . ," Django said after a long pause. "You have dinner plans? You're not dressed for dinner, exactly, but . . ."

"We could order in," she said impetuously.

"You eat Ethiopian?"

Anna smiled. "Can't say I ever have."

"Just so happens I've got a mess of leftovers in my fridge from Langano in Sherman Oaks. I'm kinda hooked on it. Be back in a flash."

Anna hadn't planned on company for dinner. In fact, Ben had called during the afternoon, but Anna had been so exhausted she could hardly talk to him.

While Django was retrieving the food, she got two bottles of Blu imported water that her father always kept stocked and brought them into the dining room. Then she cut up a pineapple for dessert. She was halfway upstairs (she planned to change into cashmere sweats) when the doorbell rang. Even from there, she could see Django's keys sitting on the marble table in the front hall. Evidently he'd locked himself out.

"Just a sec, Django!" she called, then scampered downstairs, her skimpy robe flying. She opened the heavy front door, ready to tease Django for being such an absentminded musician.

Only it wasn't Django. It was Ben.

"Hi!" she blurted nervously. "I wasn't expecting you!"

Ben eyed her up and down, taking note of the robe and chemise. "Oh no?" he asked, grinning. "If not me, who?"

"I think me." Django answered the question for him as he strode up the walk behind Ben, two shopping bags in his hands. "Is this the great Ben? We've met, I think."

He shifted the bags to one hand and stretched out his right one for Ben to shake. Ben took it without enthusiasm.

"We were just about to have dinner," Anna said by way of lame explanation. The awkwardness didn't pass, but Django looked about as loose and at ease as a man could get. "This is a great surprise."

"I called a minute ago, but there was no answer," Ben said.

Anna pointed upstairs. "My cell's in my room, sorry."

"And you're down here. With the . . . driver."

Clearly the jibe didn't bother Django, who gave Ben one of his patented no-hat salutes. "I figured since Anna never tasted Ethiopian food, I'd bring some over," he said, his Louisiana accent more acute than usual. "What say you pull up a plate and visit?"

"I don't care for Ethiopian, thanks."

Django nodded. "It's an acquired taste. Anyway, I can see that Miss Anna just got plans for the evening, so we'll do it another time. Hang in there, cowboy." Then he turned and loped down the path toward the guesthouse.

"Something about that guy . . ." Ben's eyes were still narrowed.

"My dad's out of town, he lives on the property, and he's a really good guy."

Ben kissed her softly. "Well, *this* really good guy came over with a surprise. It's parked out front. Ever seen Los Angeles at night from the Hollywood sign?"

Anna shook her head.

"You can't. It's illegal. But there's a place I know that's just as good. Go get changed."

"But I have so much to tell you," Anna exclaimed. "I went over to Apex so that Margaret could hand me my head. But the most amazing thing happened—"

Ben put a finger to Anna's lips. "Warm clothes first. We'll be outside. Then you can tell me on the way, all right?"

"To where?"

"I believe the word *surprise* is involved," he reminded her, chuckling.

Anna smiled. "I put myself in your more than capable hands."

Bundle of Contradictions

"Sorry to get you out of bed so early," Sam told Anna as they walked through her father's palatial Bel Air estate to the screening room in the back. "But in the afternoon Poppy has her work crews here doing renovation and the noise is ridiculous. I don't even come home anymore till they leave."

It was the next morning before school. Sam had invited Anna over to show her the final cut of the short film they'd made together as a school project for English class, inspired by *The Great Gatsby*. They'd shot the film the previous weekend at V's spa in Palm Springs—Sam had handled the camera work and production aspects, and Anna had written the short screenplay. They'd had friends and guests at V's play the actors and had decided to intercut real-life images to make it a kind of cinema verité. They'd filmed those this past weekend, too.

This would be Anna's first look at the finished product. She was excited and a little nervous. Writing the screenplay, which she'd titled *Three-Way*—had been a tremendous amount of fun.

"So, I spoke to Ben," Sam said as they turned down the wing that held the screening room. "I guess you two get to live happily ever after, huh?"

"We had a great time in Santa Barbara," Anna agreed. She wasn't about to add details, such as the before and after state of her former virginity. She and Sam weren't that kind of friends—at least not yet. Anna was reserving that conversation for her best friend back in New York, Cynthia Baltres.

"So are you guys super-glued at the hip?" Sam quipped.

"Not exactly." Anna thought about last night, when they'd driven up to Lake Hollywood to take in the view of the city and then gone out for a burger she didn't even want because she knew how badly that perfectly innocent dinner with Django must have appeared to Ben.

"I guess I owe you an apology, too," Sam told her as they approached the door to her father's screening room. "I talked to Adam last night."

"So I heard, and so did I. After you did," Anna said ruefully.

"You're not mad at me?"

Anna shrugged. "You didn't do it on purpose. Why should I be mad at you? Anyway, I'm having lunch with him later today."

"Be nice. He's a great guy."

"I know." Sam swung open the door to her dad's screening room. It was ministadium style, with steeply sloping seats of buttery Italian leather.

"Impressive," Anna said, taking it all in.

"Hungry?" Sam asked. "I had the cook put out a little something." She swept her hand toward the rear. By the screening booth was a linen-tablecloth-covered table supporting silver urns of coffee and tea, a stack of Krispy Kreme doughnuts large enough to feed a marine battalion, plus assorted croissants and Danishes. "It's exactly what you'd find from Craft service at a shoot. I thought it would lend an ironic touch of authenticity."

"Craft service?"

"Catering," Sam clarified. "So, take something; I'll get the film rolling. Sit in the third row. It has the best sound in the room."

Anna took the plainest doughnut she could find, poured some coffee, and slid into the third row.

"Okay, we're rolling!" Sam shouted to her. "Lights'll dim in ten seconds."

Sam bounded down the stairs and slipped into the seat next to Anna. True to her word, the lights dimmed automatically in exactly ten seconds. Then, with the room pitch-black, the film began.

"I changed the title," Sam whispered. "I hope you don't mind."

Moment by Moment. Anna read the new title as it flashed over an establishing shot of V's spa to the accompaniment of a classical solo guitar that Anna recognized as Andrés Segovia.

"Nice on the music," Anna hissed, and felt a grateful squeeze from Sam on her forearm in return. Then the actual film began, and Anna felt as nervous as if she'd just sunk her last hundred million dollars into under-writing it, though she knew the running time was prob-ably going to be less than ten minutes.

The plot was simple. There were three main charac-ters. Dan, played by their friend Parker Pinelli, came from a family that had just made a ton of money in the stock market. Mike, played by a guy they'd met at V's named Jamie, came from old-line Boston moneyed aristocracy. Both guys wanted a girl named Nina, who was a walking bundle of contradictions. Nina had been played by Dee.

As the film unfolded, Anna found herself transfixed. Sam had done a masterful job of intercutting the char-acter's monologues with actual footage from the spa as well as directing the actors. Even Dee, who Anna would have expected to be talent-free, managed to bring a cer-tain waiflike charm to the Nina role. The film ended with Mike—who'd been spurned by Nina at the end of the film—directly addressing the camera:

"People can call it passion. Or lust. Or obsession. I don't really care. When I'm with her, touching her, is the only time I feel completely alive. If you've never felt the power of that, then I feel sorry for you."

Anna remembered writing those words in her suite at V's as she had worked and reworked the conclusion of her script. She knew she was a different person now. A few days before, she'd written those words from a theoretical viewpoint. Now, a hundred hours or so later, the theoretical had become the actual, with Ben.

The film ended with another long shot of V's spa, the Segovia music dancing with the soaring song of a desert mockingbird and then being overwhelmed by that mockingbird in the same way that Mike's passion was overwhelming him. The mockingbird's warble didn't end until the screen had gone to black and the credits had rolled.

Sam clicked a couple of times on a handheld remote, and the lights in the screening room came back.

"So. Whaddaya think?" Anna could hear the nervousness in Sam's voice underneath her usual bravado.

Impulsively Anna reached over and hugged her. "I think you're a genius," she told her. "It's fantastic!"

"You really liked it?" Sam asked. "The running time is only seven minutes twenty."

"I think it's perfect. I'd love to do another one with you sometime."

Sam's smile lit up the screening room. "We'll see what we can arrange." She stood up. "I'll be right back. There's one other thing I wanted to show you. Then we can face the joy of high school." Sam scurried back into the screening booth, and the lights in the screening room again went dark as film once again rolled.

Anna gasped. Because what she was watching was film taken from the Mount St. Helens lava rock sauna at V's spa this past weekend, when Ben had burst unannounced into the sauna and Dee had claimed in front of everyone to be pregnant with Ben's baby. There was Anna, mortified by all of this. There was Susan, egging the confrontation on with a born instigator's sensibility of what would rile things up the most.

The footage stopped abruptly, and the room lights came back on. Sam stepped down from the booth. "Good thing I didn't cut *that* into our film, huh?" she asked blithely. "It would have been quite the *scandale*."

Anna felt hurt. "Why did you show me that?"

"Cards up on the table, of course," Sam told her. "Now you know you can trust me. Shall I do the honors or will you?" she asked as she took the tape out of the projection machine, threw it to the floor, and poised her foot to step on it.

"Go ahead," Anna said. Sam smiled and literally stomped on the tape until it shattered. Then she dumped the whole mess in the trash. "All gone."

"Thank God," Anna said.

"No," Sam corrected with a smile. "Thank me. After all, what are true friends for?"

"So you'll be able to come?"

"Aye-aye, sir," Anna told Ben, holding the cell phone close to her ear as a big truck rolled by on Beverly Boulevard. "As long as the captain promises that this voyage will end more satisfactorily than the last one."

"On my life."

"I'll hold you to it." Anna saw Adam pull up in front of the restaurant on his bicycle. "Ben, I've got to go," she told him. "But I look forward to it."

"Pick you up at seven, then," he said. "I miss you already."

Anna hung up just as Adam strolled up to the outdoor table she'd selected at Jerry's Deli, directly across from the famous Beverly Center indoor shopping mall. She'd offered to drive, but Adam said that he'd be more comfortable on his bicycle.

That way, Anna realized, he can get up and leave whenever he wants to and not have to drive back to school with me. In a way, I guess I can't blame him.

"Hi," she said, standing. She felt like an idiot when she offered him her hand to shake, but she did it anyway. He took it without betraying emotion, nodded somewhat curtly, and then sat down. The place was crowded—a mix of West Hollywood actor types and tourists.

"I'm glad you decided to come," she told him. "I just feel like there's a lot that hasn't been said that needs to be said."

He took the enormous Jerry's menu out of the metal holder and scanned it idly. "Stick to the mile-high pastrami," he advised her. "You won't be sorry."

But suddenly Anna's appetite was gone. Adam was such a truly decent human being. She cared about him. A lot. And though their relationship had been brief, he'd never been anything except wonderful to her. She cleared her throat. "I know Sam told you about me and Ben. . . ."

The waitress swung over to their table. Adam

ordered the pastrami. Anna settled for a buttered bagel and coffee.

"You didn't have to invite me to lunch to confirm that," Adam said. "The only thing that pisses me off is why you didn't just tell me the truth in the first place."

"I *did* tell you the truth. When I stopped seeing you, it wasn't to see him or anyone else. Then . . . things changed."

His gaze at her was jaundiced. "Come on, Anna. I'm a big boy."

"I'm telling you the truth. I wanted to be alone and figure out my life."

Adam sipped his water. "Well, evidently you figured it out pretty quickly."

Anna sighed. "I deserve that. I know I do. And I can't make any excuses. But . . . I hope when you're less upset, we can stay friends."

Adam laughed. "Come on, Anna. Can't you do better than that? 'We can stay friends'?"

"Well, I do," Anna said defensively. "You're a great guy. Who wouldn't want to be friends with you?"

The waitress brought Adam his sandwich and Anna her bagel. Clearly his appetite wasn't affected, because he took a huge bite before speaking again. "Has any guy ever said yes to, 'I hope when you're less upset, we can stay friends'?"

Anna's cheeks reddened. "Quite the cliché, huh."

"No kidding. I should get those words tattooed on my chest because I've heard them so many times. And

I've had this conversation before, too. Once in a Starbucks in Ann Arbor, once in a campground on Lake Michigan, and once outside the guys' locker room at Michigan State University just before the quarterfinals of the state high-school tournament. Not with the same girl, either. You know, I wish I'd patented that line. I'd be rich by now."

"I'm sorry, Adam. I'm just . . . I don't know what else to say."

He raised his right hand. "Waitress?"

The blond waitress saw his gesture and came over to him. Her nameplate said *Natasha*.

"*Ti gavoreet po-russki*, Natasha?"

The waitress grinned. "*Da*," she said. "*Ti Amerikanits?*"

Adam smiled at her and fired off a half minute of unintelligible Russian as Natasha nodded gravely.

"*Da. Pazalstra.* I wrap your sandwich for you." Then she looked at Anna. "This guy, he speak perfect Russian. He good guy. You be sorry someday." She patted Adam's arm, turned on her heel, and stormed away. Anna recalled that during one of their many long conversations, Adam had mentioned that he spoke "some Russian." Evidently it was more than "some."

"What'd you say to her?"

"Not, 'When you're less upset, I hope we can be friends.'"

Anna nodded. Though she'd wanted to bare her soul to Adam, to make him understand that she really hadn't planned to hurt him, she found that there was nothing else to say.

"I like you, Anna Percy. I like you a lot. But the friendship thing . . . I don't know. We'll have to see."

With that, Adam stood, picked up his sandwich, now wrapped to go, and dropped a twenty-dollar bill on the table. "For mine and yours," he said. "See ya at school."

Anna stared down at her coffee until she was sure that Adam was well on his way back to Beverly Hills High. At the moment, she didn't like herself very much at all.

Faux Sincerity

"I like this," Patrice's daughter, Mia, said as she slammed into Cammie's room without knocking and headed for the floor-length, three-way mirror. She spun around, checking out her reflection from all angles.

Cammie had been flipping through the new *Los Angeles* magazine to see if her photo had made it in that month—God knew she'd been to enough movie openings and high-profile parties in the last month to deserve it. There was a big spread on Jackson Sharpe's wedding; there was even a picture of that bitch Anna Percy with Ben Birnbaum standing with the hosts of *Good Day, L.A.,* the top-rated early morning show in the city. The hosts were identified by name, Anna and Ben as "an unidentified handsome couple."

There was nothing of Cammie.

Seething, she looked up to see Mia twirling before her mirror in a burgundy Betseyville-by-Betsey-Johnson sequined velvet miniskirt and pink Tracy Reese silk chiffon bustier. The outfit was great. The fact that Cammie had purchased it two weeks ago at Barney's and hadn't even taken it out of its box was not.

"What did you do? Sneak into my closet?" Cammie demanded.

Mia turned, hands on her narrow hips. "Shows what you know. My mom said I could try on your clothes."

Cammie folded her arms. "Well, I say you can't."

"Jeez. I was just trying to be nice," Mia muttered under her breath as she flounced out of the room, still wearing Cammie's bustier.

Cammie lay back on the stack of white and cream silk pillows atop her extra-king-size teak platform bed and sighed. Her "stepsister" had moved in a mere sixteen hours ago, and it had taken a mere sixteen minutes for Cammie to detest her.

Clark had sent his driver to pick the girl up in the valley. When they returned, he had carried in an endless number of cheap suitcases, followed by a coltish girl with choppy, flaming red hair and a petulant look. She wore low-cut cheap jeans that Cammie didn't recognize and a black T-shirt with *Teen Millionaire* sequined over her nearly nonexistent breasts. Over the tee was a mini red pleather jacket—at least Cammie thought that was what the material was called—that hideous plastic shit made to look like leather. On her feet were pink Converse All Stars with pink shoelaces. The outfit alone sufficed to make Cammie want to lose her lunch (she wasn't one of the many girls at Beverly Hills High who voluntarily sacrificed their midday meal in the BHH "Binge and Barf" club, either).

Then there was Mia's makeup. Chalk white eye shadow and black liquid eyeliner. Nothing else. Ugh.

A maid had helped Mia settle in since Patrice was at the Fox lot re-looping some dialogue for a featured role she had in the new Adam Sandler movie. From the moment they'd been introduced, Cammie had tried to simply avoid the girl. The driver had taken her to her school in the valley that morning and picked her up afterward. Meanwhile, Cammie had gone to the Beverly Hills Hotel with Dee to have espresso and see if any hot guys were wandering around. Mia had beaten her home. And evidently had sashayed into Cammie's room to do a search-and-expropriate of any clothes that struck her valley girl fancy.

Suddenly Mia reappeared in the doorway in bra and thong, flinging Cammie's outfit into the room. It landed in a heap on the thick carpeting. "That's what I get for trying to be nice? Thanks for nothing, sis!" She slammed Cammie's door so the bang put the exclamation mark at the end of the sentence. Cammie loathed slammed doors unless she was the one doing the slamming. She swung off her bed and marched down the stairs to Mia's new room, where Mia was on her bed in her underwear, reading a screenplay.

"Go away."

Cammie stepped inside.

Mia briefly looked up. "What do you want?"

"I want to set a few ground rules. One, don't come into my room without my permission, ever. Two, never

borrow my stuff without asking. Three, I never let anyone borrow my clothes, so don't ask. Stay out of my
way and I'll happily stay out of yours. Are we clear?"

"Sure," Mia replied. Then she looked back down at
the script.

"I'm talking to you, you brat." Cammie stepped to
the bed and yanked the script out of her hands, shut-
ting it in the process. It was a new spec by a very
famous screenwriter whom her father happened to rep-
resent. Cammie knew for a fact that a studio was currently casting the project because it seemed as if half
the girls at Beverly Hills High were auditioning for the
lead teen role. The script itself, though, was top secret.
Even the stars hadn't seen it.

"Where did you get this?"

Mia looked unsettled. "Around."

"From my father's office downstairs?" Cammie
demanded. Clark had a home office where he sometimes worked on the weekends if he didn't feel like
driving to Westwood. It was as disorganized and free-
form as his Apex office was neat. Screenplays and tele-
plays covered every square inch of free space that
wasn't his chair or the spot on his desk where he'd rest
his feet. The maids had strict orders not to enter, even
if they knew there was a six-day-old uneaten lunch
moldering away on the floor. Even Cammie stayed out
of it.

"Whatever," Mia mumbled. "My mom said it was
okay."

"You are never, ever, *ever* to go in there. Do you hear me?"

"I didn't do anything wrong! Why are you being so mean to me? I just got here!" Mia got up and padded into her private bath.

Though she felt like busting down the door and slapping the stupid girl silly, Cammie was far too smart to succumb to such an impulse. The fact was, when her father found out that Patrice's daughter had snuck into his home office and taken a top secret script, her ass would be fresh-cut grass, and she'd be on a slow bus back to the valley in no time.

Bye-bye, Mia. Valley Village or bust.

"Your father is in a meeting," Gerard told Cammie. "Can I get you anything, Cammie? Water, coffee?"

"Coffee, but brew a fresh pot," Cammie insisted. "What meeting?"

"You'd have to ask him," Gerard said. "Hang out. I'll be right back with your coffee. Two percent milk and Equal, right?"

Cammie sat in the leather chair by Gerard's work-station and pretended to leaf through *Variety* until Gerard had turned a corner on the way to the office kitchen. Then she walked the few paces down to her father's office. The door was partially open. She peeked in: there was her father, practically knee to knee with Anna Percy. Was the world conspiring to ruin her day?

Cammie pushed open the door and stepped into her

dad's office. "Hi, Anna," she said, oozing faux sincerity. "How nice to see you."

Anna looked up. "Hi," she said.

Clark stared at his daughter, then at Anna. He gave Anna an "excuse me" look, got up, and went to the door and took Cammie outside.

"What's up?"

"Just something at home."

"Did Gerard tell you to barge in here?"

Cammie felt herself redden. No one could humiliate her quite the way her father could.

"I'm really busy, Cammie," her father went on. "If you need to speak with me, we'll be done in around fifteen minutes. Tell Gerard to make you some coffee."

Her father was *dismissing* her? Impossible.

"I just thought you'd want to know," Cammie began, head held high, "that Patrice's spawn stole Bradley O'Keefe's new screenplay."

"Why the hell did you let her into my office?" her father blasted, glaring at her.

"I wasn't even there, okay?" Cammie shot back. "I caught her with it in her room."

Her father sighed. "I'll deal with it when I get home. Is that all?"

Cammie tossed her hair off her face. "Mia has to go, Dad. I'm serious."

Her father put an arm around her shoulders and spoke quietly. "I said, I'll deal with it. She's not going anywhere."

"But—"

"She's fourteen. Buck up. You didn't write that script."

"She's loathsome."

"You know nothing about her, or what she's been through, or what the situation is now."

Cammie could see Gerard returning with her coffee, so she whirled back to her father. "How could I know anything about Mia? The bitch won't have a conversation with me!"

"Got some advice for you, Cammie," her father murmured in her ear. "Grow the hell up." Then he made a big show of hugging her goodbye, stepped back into his office, and closed the door emphatically.

Gerard held a paper coffee cup out to her. "Your coffee, Cammie?"

<u>HERMOSA</u> <u>BEACH</u>

FADE IN:

CHYME LANGLEY, 17, the kind of bikini-clad blonde that makes all little girls aspire to move to California, and her boyfriend, CRUISE PEREZ, 18, a bad boy from the wrong side of the tracks, walk hand in hand down the sun-swept beach.

CRUISE

I'm not going to dishonor your father. He's been too good to me.

                    CHYME
All we did was fall in love. It's not a
crime!

                    CRUISE
Your father owns Hermosa Beach Hotel,
Chyme. And you've fallen in love with
the maintenance man's son. In this town
that's not awkward. That's a felony.

Anna sat on the living room couch, feet tucked
under her, reading the pilot script to *Hermosa Beach*
that had been messengered to her dad's house. Her
mind still reeled at the notion that Clark Sheppard in
essence wanted her to be his protégé and help out on
the show.

"People think the bucks in this town are in movies,"
he'd told her that day in his office. "But that's bullshit.
TV rules."

Anna had never given it much thought one way or
the other. Aside from the one short screenplay she'd
written for the film with Sam, she'd never considered a
career in show business. Teaching literature at a small
New England college had always seemed a more likely
endeavor. But for some reason, Clark seemed to find
her innocence a positive. That her reference points
would be great works of literature rather than modern
movies struck him as a plus.

There was a brief cover note that came with the

material Clark had sent over. In it Clark explained how the producers had sold the show to the network as a modern retelling of John Milton's *Paradise Lost,* with the characters of Chyme and Cruise representing Adam and Eve tempted by a snake, Alexandra. At first Anna thought he was joking, but evidently he was totally serious. The unspoken message was that in Los Angeles, *Hermosa Beach* passed as literature.

Anna read a few more pages, then the melodic chimes of the doorbell rang. She went to open it. Django stood there, two large brown paper bags in hand.

"Smell." He held one bag up to her nose. The most amazing, exotic spices wafted from the warm bag—Anna couldn't place them.

"Whatever it is, it smells heavenly."

"And tastes even better. Since our Ethiopian dinner got called last night on account of jealousy, I thought we'd try again. I know it's still early, but are you up for it?"

Anna let the "on account of jealousy" remark pass and waved Django in. "That was thoughtful of you. Ben's coming at seven, though."

"Weren't nothin', Miss Anna," Django drawled in his best "aw, shucks" accent. "Pick your locale."

"How about here," Anna decided. "I've got a video to watch, if you can get my dad's TV to function. I think that's called a working meal."

As she got plates and silver and he got the television

working, she explained the new direction her internship had taken—how she was supposed to assist Clark Sheppard on *Hermosa Beach.*

"I'm game if you are," Django said. "But truth is, I don't watch network TV."

"That's the truly funny thing." Anna put the pilot into the combination VCR and DVD player. "Neither do I. It seems as if in this town, if you have no interest in show business, show business is all the more interested in you."

Anna sat next to Django on the couch, where he'd set fragrant flat, round bread on their plates. Between them was another piece of this bread covered with little mounds of various foods—mashed chick peas, greens, beets, potatoes, and a few other things she couldn't identify. Django showed her how to break off a small piece of the soft bread and use it to scoop up a bite of the food.

"No silverware involved," he added solemnly. He pulled off a small piece of bread, grabbed some of what looked like chicken, and held it out to Anna. She leaned forward and he popped it into her mouth. It was spicy and sour and completely unlike anything she'd ever tasted before.

"That is . . . amazing!"

"Now you know why I drive over the hill to Sherman Oaks to get this stuff at Langano twice a week. There are other Ethiopian places south on Fairfax, but they don't compare," Django said, laughing. "Dang if I ain't addicted." He popped a bite into his own mouth. "Well, let's see the show, girl."

She started the pilot. The theme music rocked, and they watched a gorgeous blond teen girl running on the beach in front of a small upscale hotel. Then a gorgeous, shirtless Latino teen guy repaired a window shade in one of the hotel rooms. He stepped onto the balcony and watched the girl run. There were quick shots of a few other people—all equally gorgeous. Then the title of the show and some credits flashed on the screen.

"High art. I think I'm remembering why I hardly watch any TV," Django said between bites. "Although Hermosa Beach is beautiful."

"It's a real place?" Anna asked, astonished.

"Yep, south of the airport, between Manhattan Beach and Redondo Beach. Big nightlife scene, beautiful sand, huge pier. A good hang."

Twenty minutes later Anna was licking chicken juice from her fingers and enjoying the food and the company immensely—far more than the TV pilot. When the blond hotel heiress—Chyme—was stealing a forbidden kiss with the Latino son of the maintenance man—Cruise—Django shook his head. "Are they giving Shakespeare any credit for this retread?"

Anna cocked her head at him and hit the pause button. "It's supposed to be like Milton. Don't you believe in love?"

He sat back and studied her. "Do you?"

She nodded.

"You in it now?" He waited patiently for her answer.

Was she in love with Ben? She certainly cared about him. Loved the way he made her feel. Loved his hands on her and his lips on hers and—

"You're blushin', girl," Django said with a sly half grin.

"No, I'm not." But that only made more color rise to her cheeks. "I'm *not.*"

"You are so busted!" Django hooted. At that moment the door chimed. "Saved by the bell," he added, laughing harder as she headed for the door.

She glanced at her watch. Seven o'clock.

It should be . . .

She opened the door. And it was.

"Ben! Hi! You're right on time!" She wrapped her arms around his neck and kissed him, making sure Django could see. So that neither guy would get the wrong idea.

Whatever that was.

Semester at Sea

"This time will be totally different, I promise."

Ben and Anna stood on the deck of Ben's father's yacht, the *Nip-n-Tuck III*. It was docked in Marina del Rey at the same slip where Anna had last seen it on New Year's Eve. At the time, Anna had considered it the most romantic night of her life. Until Ben had abandoned her at the boatyard at three o'clock in the morning and she'd had to call Django to rescue her. But it was different now. Everything was different.

"My plan is to erase the first time on this vessel from your memory," Ben said softly, gently pushing some windblown hair off her face. "I could spend forever making it up to you. Gladly." He kissed her. "Okay. Now I have to get her ready to go. Don't do a thing except stand there and look beautiful."

Ben readied the boat while Anna enjoyed the salt air from the bow. She heard Ben start the engines and watched him untie the moorings; then he eased the yacht out of the slip and they cleared the marina. Soon the engines opened up, and they were steaming out into the endless Pacific. Finally Ben killed the motor and joined her, snaking his arms around her from behind. Tall as she was, he was taller, and his head rested just above hers.

"Nice?"

"Very."

He turned her around. His hands traveled down to her waist, then lower, holding her fast. "Remember this?" The kiss he gave her heated her right through the down vest and jeans she'd pulled from her closet. And yes, it did remind her of the last time they'd been on this boat together, when she'd felt as if her entire life was new and wonderful and dangerous.

"It's warmer down below. In the cabin," Ben suggested, his voice low.

He led her down the steep steps and into the cabin. He kissed her until she couldn't breathe. Removed her down vest. Her Ralph Lauren Blue Label cashmere turtleneck. Her handmade white silk camisole from a darling little shop on the Boulevard St. Michel in Paris. Slipped her out of her jeans. Then Ben pulled off his own sweater and gently kissed Anna onto the bed's ruby velvet quilt. And then . . .

And then . . .

The emotions of her last time on this boat came flooding over her. She was powerless to fend them off. Anna put her hand gently against Ben's chest. He was breathing hard. There was a question in his eyes.

"I'm sorry," she whispered. "I keep thinking about last time."

"New memories, Anna. We're making new memories," Ben whispered, reaching behind her back for the narrow clasp of her lace bra.

"I want that, too, Ben," Anna insisted. "Just . . . not this place."

He flopped over onto his back, a forearm thrown over his forehead. "Don't you think that if I could go back and do everything differently, I would?"

"I'm not trying to punish you. I'm just telling you how I feel."

He rolled onto one hip and gazed at her. "I'm not much good at saying how I feel. In fact, I suck at it."

"I read somewhere that women bond facing each other and talking and men bond facing a sporting event and yelling for their team," Anna said, apropos of nothing but her own discomfort.

"Good to know I'm not unique. If there was any way I could make it up to you, you know I would."

"You don't have to."

"Let's get under the covers," Ben said. He slid the quilt down on one side and both of them climbed in. Ben lay on his back; Anna put her head somewhere in the vicinity of his heart.

"I wish we could just sail out into the Pacific," Ben murmured into her hair. "Keep going and never come back."

"Does Princeton offer a semester-at-sea program?" Anna joked.

"Don't know and don't care."

Anna lifted her head so that she could see his eyes. "When are you going back to school?"

"Soon."

Soon? Anna knew that Ben's second semester had started and that he'd missed a few days of it already. It wasn't like a person could take freshman year at Princeton casually. She wondered if that was part of the reason she was holding back: her knowledge that soon he'd have to leave.

"How much school have you missed?"

Ben groaned. "Anna, we came out here to get away from stress, not bring it with us."

He was right. Why, why, why couldn't she learn to just *be* in the moment?

"Sorry," she whispered, then leaned down to kiss him. His arms circled her. She kissed his neck, down his chest. She heard him groan.

"Don't start what you're not going to finish," he said hoarsely.

Anna was determined to stay in the now. Not the past, when Ben had abandoned her on the boat. And not the murky future, when he'd leave for college.

She raised herself over him and whispered in his ear: "Race you to the finish."

He rolled her over and pinned her down with his strong hands. He smiled down into her eyes. "You're on."

Anna awoke with a start. The same boat, the same bed, the same no one beside her. Oh my God, it was happening all over again! She threw off the covers, not thinking about how naked she was, and jumped out of bed . . .

Just as Ben came down the cabin stairs with two steaming cups of fresh-brewed coffee from the boat's tiny galley. "If you greet me in that outfit, I'll bring you coffee anytime."

"I thought you were . . ."

She felt too stupid and couldn't finish the sentence.

"Gone? You really thought that?"

She didn't answer him. Instead she crawled back into bed. He handed her the coffee and sat next to her. "I'm so sorry, Anna. I swear to you, it will never, ever happen again."

He looked so sad, so earnest. She nodded and gratefully sipped the coffee. What they'd shared for the past couple of hours had been amazing. She'd fallen asleep with a contented smile on her lips. How could she wake up with the same old fears?

A memory, long buried, flitted into her mind. Of her father, there one day and then . . . gone. Her mother wouldn't talk about it. In fact, it was nearly a year until she informed her daughters that she and their father had gone through a very civil divorce and Jonathan Percy was now living in Beverly Hills, California, his hometown. She wanted to tell Ben about this. Yet something stopped her. For all her insight into "bonding," Anna knew little about intimacy. God knew she hadn't learned it from the *This Is How We Do Things*

Big Book, East Coast WASP edition. Sharing something so personal was number one in that apocryphal book's "Thou Shalt Nots."

So she didn't. Instead she sipped her coffee and tried to enjoy the moment for what it was.

Ninety minutes later they'd docked at Marina del Rey, secured the boat, and made their way back to Ben's parked car. Ben cranked the heater, gallantly making sure that the vents were pointed at Anna as they pulled out of the marina's parking lot. "Have fun?"

"It was wonderful," Anna assured him. She kissed her fingertips and touched them to his cheek as her eyes flicked to the clock on his dashboard. Nearly midnight. Theoretically there was school the next day.

On the boat ride back to the marina Anna had filled Ben in on how she'd be interning for Clark Sheppard at the Apex agency. And now, as they drove back to Beverly Hills, she found herself thinking about it . . . as well as the look Cammie had fired in her direction when Clark had summarily dismissed his daughter from his office.

Evidently the subject was on Ben's mind, too. Out of nowhere he said, "Listen, watch your elegant ass around Cammie Sheppard, okay?"

"I have no interest in giving her a moment's thought."

"She's capable of pretty much anything."

"You're aware that she still wants you back," Anna pointed out.

"She knows I'm not interested."

Something made Anna press the point as Ben sped north on Lincoln Boulevard toward the 10 freeway. "You're the one who said she's capable of anything. She could hop on a jet and show up at Princeton."

"Don't care, Anna." He pressed a button on the dashboard, and cool jazz filled his Nissan's interior.

"Sorry about the sound system," Ben apologized. "This is a rental car, remember."

"It doesn't matter. The sound. But going back to school—you must think about it," Anna said. She twisted around so she could see him.

"Only because you keep bringing it up."

"But school is—"

"Can't we just be here, now? Can't we?"

She sat back. Why wouldn't he talk about Princeton? It wasn't like it was a state secret. The crisis at his house was over, he'd told her. Why was he still hanging around Beverly Hills?

"What happens when I do go back, Anna?" he asked, staring hard at the road.

"What do you mean?"

"I mean, the Contessa and the Southern-Fried Chauffeur."

Anna's jaw flapped open. "Are you talking about Django?"

"The way he looks at you—"

"Ben. We're *friends.*"

"Close friends?" Ben probed. "Close personal friends?"

Heat came to Anna's face. "I don't deserve that."

His hands gripped the steering wheel. "The idea of being on the other side of the country, being without you, and he lives right there, it's just . . ."

Anna put a slender hand on Ben's thigh. "Django and I are *friends,*" she said again.

He nodded, then cranked up the music. They didn't talk again until they reached her father's house, where he parked in the circular driveway and took her into his arms. "Hey. Sorry about before. I just care about you so damn much."

"It's okay." She kissed him softly. "It's forgotten."

He walked her to the door and kissed her again. She thanked him for an incredible evening, then watched him drive away. And out of the corner of her eye, she couldn't help noticing that the lights in Django's guesthouse were still illuminated.

Nice-ta-meetcha

"**S**o I was wondering if you might stop by the *Well* office sometime this afternoon so we could do an interview."

"I don't know . . . ," Anna said, stifling an unintentional yawn. "I mean, I just—"

"Come on," cajoled Juliet Dinkins, editor in chief of the Beverly Hills High newspaper, the *Well.* "The whole school already knows that you're working on *Hermosa Beach* anyway. It's not like it's some big secret."

"I didn't tell anyone."

Juliet laughed. "Welcome to L.A."

Anna had been eating lunch alone at one of the picnic tables in the quadrangle. Tired from her late night with Ben, she hoped the yogurt and fruit she was about to eat would help perk her up. She had been reading *Love and Death in the American Novel,* the seminal—in more ways than one—collection of essays by the late literary critic Leslie Fiedler and spooning vanilla yogurt into her mouth when Juliet had come running over to her, steno notebook in hand.

"Look. I'll make it easy for you. I'll give you the questions in advance," Juliet said, her lustrous dark hair glinting in the noonday sun. "Is it true that Clark Sheppard picked you from out of a thousand applicants? What exactly are you going to be doing? What kind of connections did you use to get this gig? What's it like on the set of the show? Is Scott Stoddard, the star, really gay, or is that just a rumor? Can we come down to the beach to do an interview with the cast?"

Anna shook her head, thinking that this was insane. She hadn't told anyone about her new gig at Apex—not even Sam. But word had spread like wildfire, which meant the most likely explanation was that Cammie had gotten the news from her father after Anna departed. Surely Cammie would have demanded to know why Anna was in her dad's office. Surely Clark Sheppard had told her.

However the word had leaked, kids were coming up to her—kids she didn't even know!—all through her morning classes to either offer congratulations or wheedle favors. There were plenty of young actors at Beverly Hills High; each of them instantly realized that Anna could be their ticket to a guest TV appearance or, at the very least, an audition.

"I can't answer those questions," Anna told Juliet.

Juliet's eyebrows shot up. "Can't or won't?"

Anna polished her apple on her camel-colored cashmere sweater. "There are dozens of kids at this school who've been on TV or in a film. I just don't see why my internship is of any particular interest."

"Come on, Anna. Anyone with a pretty face, buff biceps, or a parent in the business can be on TV," Juliet said. "But *Hermosa Beach* is supposed to be the hot new show. There are billboards for it all over town. You're working on it, and for one of the most powerful people in this town. In other words, Anna, you hit the Powerball jackpot, even if you're too naive to know it, which I somehow don't think you are. So about the interview—"

"Juliet, listen. I haven't even had my first day on the show yet," Anna interrupted. "And I can't do an interview without clearing it with Mr. Sheppard."

Juliet stood. "Whatever. If you don't cooperate, I might have to do the story without you. And you know how misleading that can be. It might even come out wrong—like maybe you got the gig because you're doing 'Mr. Sheppard.'"

"Because that's just the kind of smut Beverly Hills High is apt to allow into their newspaper . . ."

Juliet shook her hair off her shoulders. "You may have made it to the top of the Beverly Hills High social ladder in record time, but never doubt my ability to get things done my way," she said as she smiled confidently and walked away.

Unbelievable. A high school newspaper editor was threatening to do a libelous exposé on her? What was wrong with this town?

As soon as Juliet was gone, Sam rushed over and sat down. "She wants to interview you," she guessed. "For the paper."

"More like she wants to write something juicy enough for her tear sheets to make an impression when she applies for her next summer internship," Anna guessed.

"She's a barracuda. But if you give her the interview, she probably won't bite hard enough to draw blood."

Anna almost laughed. "Am I supposed to find that reassuring?"

Sam waved an airy hand. "Don't even worry about it. I can sit on her if you want. I know things she definitely doesn't want known by the general public." Sam leaned closer. "So how'd you pull this one off?"

"I went to Apex to talk to Margaret—"

"You were so sure she was going to fire you."

"She did, he didn't. I think it's some kind of power struggle. Anyway, Cammie's dad walked in; ten minutes later he was asking me to intern for him."

Sam looped some glossy, perfectly-streaked-by-Raymond chestnut hair behind her ear, exposing her new eighteen-karat-gold double-tier drop earrings with aquamarine and peridot from the Lauren Harper Collection. "So, how pissed off did that make Margaret?"

"On a scale of one to ten, I'd say she was pushing eleven," Anna admitted.

"Good!" Sam laughed. "Guess who's pushing twelve?"

"Cammie." Anna groaned.

"Right on the first guess."

Anna spooned some yogurt into her mouth. "I'm

not getting involved in her latest drama. If she's angry at anyone, it should be at her father, not me. Besides, according to her father, she wouldn't want my job even if she could have it."

"True enough, but—hold on." Sam stood and waved her arms, trying to get the attention of a blue-jacketed man in his forties looking uncertainly around the quadrangle. "Hey! Over here!"

The man heard Sam, turned and waved in her direction, and came trotting over. "Leslie Newsom?" the guy asked.

"That's me," Sam confirmed as Anna looked on, baffled.

"Lunch delivery." The man handed her a plastic bag from a French restaurant named Le Morvan and then Sam quickly signed a receipt—Anna could see that she signed it "Leslie N." Sam tipped the deliveryman ten bucks. He gave her ten bucks' worth of thanks and left.

Sam opened the bag and extracted two plastic-plate-shaped containers, a bottle of red juice, and utensils. "Power Eating," she confided to Anna. "Don't tell *anyone.*"

"What's Power Eating?" So often Anna—who'd traveled all over the world—felt like Los Angeles was an alien universe, where she needed a full-time cultural guide in order to understand the natives.

Sam took the plastic top off one of the containers and sniffed it. "Ugh. Rabbit food. It's like the Zone, but better. They cook all the food you eat and deliver it to you four times a day. You never have to shop and you never have to cook. But the best part is they deliver it in bags from fake restaurants so no one would suspect you're on it." She forked into an already cut-up chicken breast, put it to her lips, and tasted it. "God, that sucks."

"Why don't you just eat regular food?" Anna asked.

"I woke up today, I looked in the mirror, and I almost barfed," Sam said. She held up a hand quickly. "And please don't start with the 'you look fine' bullshit. I'm a cow. So I had my dad's assistant call Power Eating for me, and I told her to register me under the name Leslie Newsom. Whoever she is." She took a bite of green salad. "Bleech! This tastes like ass."

Anna had to laugh. She really did like the girl, even if Sam did keep some strange company sometimes. "One more question. How'd the school paper get its name? The *Well*? That's kind of strange."

Sam speared another cube of chicken and forked it into her mouth. "There's crude oil under our high school. And a working oil well. Up behind the maintenance yards. That big building, covered with paintings of flowers?"

Anna's jaw fell open. "You're kidding."

"Nope. Turns out Jed Clampett could have done his hunting out here."

"Jed Clampett?" For the umpteenth time since she'd arrived in L.A., Anna felt like an idiot.

"*Beverly Hillbillies*? Sixties sitcom? Mirror image to Paris Hilton's *The Simple Life*?"

"I am totally lost," Anna admitted.

"And you're going to work in TV?" Sam smiled sadly. "Nothing makes any sense in this town. Welcome to Hollywood."

The character of Mike walked across the desert floor—the sound was good enough to pick up the rhythmic *crunch-crunch* of his steps. Then he turned, crossed his arms, and addressed the camera.

"People can call it passion. Or lust. Or obsession. I don't really care. When I'm with her, touching her, is the only time I feel completely alive. If you've never felt the power of that, then I feel sorry for you."

He held his gaze steady, focused on something in the distance. Then he turned and walked out of the frame, so that the camera took in the expanse of the Palm Springs desert—the lifeless landscape and the soaring sandstone mountain. Sam had made a last-minute edit at Anna's suggestion: rather than ending with another long shot of Veronique's spa, the last image was the glorious expanse of the desert itself. The Segovia music came up and mixed with the song of the desert mockingbird until the mockingbird overwhelmed the guitar entirely.

Then the credits started to roll: *Directed by: Samantha Sharpe. Written by: Anna Percy.* And a huge, rolling wave of applause and whoops swept through Mrs. Breckner's English class.

As the lights came up, Anna could see that even Mrs. Breckner and Dee were clapping. In fact, the only person who wasn't was Cammie.

Mrs. Breckner nodded at Sam, then at Anna. "Really fine work on *Gatsby*. Maybe this is the start of something great for the two of you."

"We're already on to our next project," Sam said. "This one's a feature called *Three-Way*. Anna's in the middle of the screenplay. My dad's financing, and we'll be shooting in the spring."

Electric excitement swept through the classroom. The five girls who considered themselves "actors" (the term *actress*, Anna had learned, was gauche) sat up straighter, or stuck their breasts out, or swung their hair—anything to attract attention. It was one thing for Sam to do a student film and quite another for her to be working on a feature—however low budget it might turn out to be—financed by one of the biggest movie stars in the world, her father.

All of which was fine, from Anna's point of view. Except for the fact that she had no idea what Sam was talking about.

"Tell us more," called Heather Chasen, who wore a geometric Marc Jacobs mini and had drawn fake lashes below her real ones for a retro Twiggy look. "Does this have anything to do with Anna working on *Hermosa Beach*?"

Others started calling out questions: How many roles would there be? When would auditions be? When could they see a copy of the script?

Anna shot Sam a look that conveyed, she hoped, her shock. Sam was clearly unperturbed by it. "As soon as possible, we'll let you know," she said smoothly. Then the bell rang, but instead of dashing for the exits, half the class gathered around Anna and Sam.

"I didn't know Sam and Anna were working on a feature, did you?" Dee asked as she and Cammie left the classroom.

"Guess what? I don't care," Cammie said.

Tiny Dee had to walk double time to keep up with Cammie's long strides. "Just remember, animosity turns loose free radicals. And this isn't a theory. It was in the Monday Health section of the *Los Angeles Times*. I think."

"Dee?"

"Yes?

"Be quiet." Cammie was in no mood to hear any of Dee's theories on life, health, or the new age. She knew it was but three sentences from animosity and free radicals to the therapeutic nature of high colonics. But the only person she wanted to get a high colonic right now—preferably with sulfuric acid—was her so-called friend Sam. How could she be working on a feature with the A-word and not even mention it? Where were her loyalties?

"Stevie!" Dee exclaimed, waving to a guy walking toward them. Cammie didn't recognize him. Which meant he didn't go to BHH, where she knew everyone who was anyone.

When the guy reached Dee, he kissed her and kept an arm looped around her tiny shoulders. "Thought I'd come check it out," the guy said with a heavy New York accent. The word *thought* came out like the word *taught*.

Dubious grasp on diction notwithstanding, Cammie had to admit he was hot, whoever he was, though in a trying-too-hard kind of way. He was tall and lanky, with jet black hair that fell forward almost over his cheek-bones. And he wore regulation rock-and-roll black—black jeans, black tee, black leather jacket. The pants had to go. But other than that, he was quite the tasty treat.

"This is Stevie Novellino," Dee told Cammie. "From New York."

"Brooklyn," Stevie corrected.

"Brooklyn," Dee echoed. "He plays guitar for Border Cross. You know, the band my dad's producing? They're in town to do a show tomorrow. At the Hollywood Bowl."

"Opening for . . . ?" Cammie asked, since she'd never heard of Border Cross.

"Beck," Stevie said. "You know Beck?"

Cammie smiled. "He's a client of a friend of mine."

"You should come 'n check it out tomorrow night," Stevie went on, shaking hair out of his eyes.

"Stevie's band just got signed to Sony," Dee reported excitedly. "And my dad's producing the new CD. Isn't that cool? We met the last time I was in New York. My dad introduced us."

"Wow," Cammie deadpanned. But her sarcasm was clearly lost on both Dee and this guy, who was evidently her new squeeze.

"I know, it's so cool!" Dee chirped. She stood on tiptoe to give Stevie a kiss. He turned it into a full-on make-out session, as if Cammie had nothing better to do than to stand there in her Badgley Mischka baby blue suede boots and watch this seventh-grade-cool twelfth-grade-sad suck-face fest.

In fact, as the kiss crossed from affectionate to disgusting, Cammie fumed anew. What was *happening?* Why was this the first time that she was hearing about this guy Stevie Novellino? Dee always confided in her, at least in the past. Was Dee joining the Sam express that was pulling away from her, too?

"When you two are done swallowing each other's spit . . ." Cammie interjected.

Dee broke the kiss and nuzzled into Stevie's chest. "Yeah?"

There was only one solution for the disquiet and anger that she felt. Retail therapy.

"Dee, say goodbye to your new friend," Cammie told her. "We're going shopping."

"Oh gosh, I can't!" Dee exclaimed. "Stevie and I are going out on David Geffen's yacht. I mean, we already promised, so . . . Did you want to come?"

"I'm busy," Cammie snapped.

"With what?"

Cammie's voice dropped to a whisper, which was what she always did when she was furious. *"Shopping."*

God, could this day get any worse?

Stevie said goodbye ("Nice-ta-meetcha"); then he and

Dee took off. Meanwhile, Cammie decided to wait for Sam. She'd find out what was going on. She'd lure Sam back to her side. They'd go shopping and spend inordinate amounts of money. Then everything would be—

"Hey, Cammie!"

Cammie turned. Sam was coming toward her. And she was arm in arm with Adam Flood.

Which meant it wasn't the time to ream Sam out, Cammie quickly decided. No reason for Adam to think that she was a coldhearted bitch. So Cammie gave Sam a big hug. "I waited for you to tell you how great your film was," she exclaimed. "Magnificently shot. Adam, you really missed something. You have to ask Sam to show you. It's wonderful."

Sam beamed. "Thanks."

"So where are you two going?" Cammie asked pleasantly.

"Bev's," Sam said, which, Cammie knew, meant the Beverly Hills Hotel. Cammie, Sam, and Dee hung out there the way kids in say, Kansas, might hang out at the local Taco Bell. "Adam's never been, can you believe it? And his basketball practice got canceled. Want to come with?"

"I'd love to, but I have to meet a friend," Cammie said, making sure the way she said it intimated that "friend" equaled hot.

"Got a new guy?" Adam asked easily.

"Always," Cammie said, laughing as if she didn't have a care in the world.

"Well, if you change your mind," Sam offered, backing away with Adam. "Call me tonight; we'll talk."

"Sure. Have a great time, you two."

Now it was Sam and Adam's turn to walk away and for Cammie's blood pressure to shoot skyward once again. Sam Sharpe and Adam Flood? Arm in arm? What happened to Adam licking his wounds over losing Anna? She remembered that Sam had told her how on New Year's Eve she and Adam had swapped some spit. But that was all. Now was Sam moving in like the pear-shaped vulture she was to pick up the pieces of the body before they rotted away entirely?

In any case, this was the first afternoon in a long time—maybe forever—that Dee and Sam had both made plans without consulting Cammie.

What was going on here? Who the hell did they think they were?

She picked up her cell and dialed home. Mia answered. "Yeah?"

"That's how people answer the phone in 818? 'Yeah'?" Cammie asked.

"What do you want?"

God, the girl was impossible. But Cammie wasn't the type to fly solo. Mia was better than nothing. "Wait outside," she snapped. "And I'll pick you up. The wicked stepsister is taking you shopping."

Cheap and Chic

C lark Sheppard's driver pulled the pearl gray
Mercedes up to the front of a white beachfront
hotel. Facing the street was a small, understated awning
that sheltered a double glass door. The only thing that
identified this place as a hotel was a small brass plaque
by the doors. Anna had to squint to read it: *Hermosa
Beach Inn. Established 1939.*

Anna was in the back, next to Cammie's father. The
chauffeur came around and opened her door. Anna slid
out, then Mr. Sheppard. He didn't bother to acknowledge his driver's existence as he led Anna to the front
doors.

"This is the place?" Anna asked.

Clark nodded. "Used to be the Seaside Manor. They
sold it and were about to renovate when we took it over
for the show. Worked out perfectly. We're able to have
our production offices on-set. We shoot inside the
hotel and outside on the beach. Wait until you see the
other side."

At the front door they were checked in at a security

desk, then Clark led Anna inside. The lobby was done in white and yellow, dotted with sun-bleached white-blond tables and handmade carpets of muted beach scenes. The furniture was of the same white-blond wood, with cushions of yellow and white. There were opaque vases on every table, holding slender stalks of white orchids, and a white grand piano in one corner. At one end was a Moroccan-style fireplace, with two neat piles of firewood stacked on either side.

It looked, for all practical purposes, like a working hotel lobby. Except for the glaring television lights, cameras, and production people scurrying around as though the take that they were about to do was the most important thing in the world to accomplish properly.

Clark stopped to watch, so Anna did, too. Huge lights were being focused carefully on the actress who played Chyme, the hotel owner's daughter. She wore a white minidress and strappy heels, and her blond hair fell in a waterfall down her back. Sitting on a folding chair close by was a brunette nearly as beautiful as Chyme. She wore what Anna recognized as a Versace dress, very colorful, slit at the sides to the waist. Her neckline vee'd all the way down to her navel. Her fingernails were long and scarlet. A makeup person dabbed at her face with powder.

"They've got at least another half hour of setup. Come on. And be careful of the cables," Clark warned Anna as they stepped over the snaking lines and made their way to a wing of the inn that had evidently been converted to a suite of production offices.

"First stop, the writers' room," Clark explained. "Sit down and listen up; you'll get a feel for what's going on with the show."

The door was open, so Anna followed Clark into a long conference room not half the size of the gargantuan conference room at Apex. And not nearly so scenic. There were no windows. On each of the two long walls hung three white boards, and on the short walls were two of the same kind of boards. On the shelf of each white board was an assortment of colored erasable markers.

That was it. No artwork, no posters, no nothing. The lighting was fluorescent, and the whole room smelled of stale coffee. The table itself was a mess, covered with notebooks, scripts, old newspapers, and half-eaten sandwiches. Around the table sat half a dozen writers, four men and two women. They all looked to be under the age of forty.

A short but very cute guy in a baseball cap was pacing, addressing the group, even though he looked like he was the youngest one there. He took a brief moment to utter a deferential greeting to Mr. Sheppard, who didn't bother to introduce Anna. Clark sat, so Anna did, too.

"Okay," said the short guy in the baseball cap. "Chyme is intimidated by Alexandra's old money confidence, yada, yada, yada. Big fucking deal. But where's Cruise fit into this equation? Why does Chyme feel so fucking threatened? Why the fuck does Alexandra scare her, really?"

A few writers offered some responses, all liberally peppering even the most ordinary sentence with the word *fuck*. Anna couldn't make any sense out of the conversation, other than to decide that a TV writers' room had to be the most profane place in the universe. But eventually she caught on to the story—the brunette actress she'd seen in the hotel lobby was East Coast rich Alexandra. She and Chyme were going to be in a love triangle with Cruise. The writers were trying to figure out how to make this triangle work.

After about forty-five minutes—in which the word *fuck* was uttered at least a hundred times and not a single sentence had been written on the white board—the staff took a break. They fled the room quickly, except for the young guy who had been running the discussion. He walked over to Clark and Anna.

"Danny, how's it going?" Mr. Sheppard asked, shaking his hand.

"Great, can'tcha tell? A million-four in salaries and they've got nothing," the guy said. His friendly brown eyes fixed on Anna. "Hi, I'm Danny Bluestone."

"Danny's our boy genius co–exec producer," Mr. Sheppard explained.

Anna frowned. "Sorry?"

"Guy in charge of this room. If the show tanks, so does he," Mr. Sheppard translated. "Danny, I want you to meet my new intern, Anna Percy. Her pedigree is just about as snooty as the one you cooked up for Alexandra."

Danny shook Anna's hand. "Nice to meet you." He grinned at her. "Actually, you look like you could *play* Alexandra."

"I'm not an actress," Anna assured him.

"Did you see Pegasus out there?"

Anna's brow furrowed. "Sorry?"

"Pegasus Patton, she's playing Alexandra," he explained. "The brunette in the lobby?"

"She's hot right now," Mr. Sheppard added. "Just came off an indie film with Nicole Kidman that's showing at Sundance in a couple of weeks. She's an Apex client."

Anna nodded politely, though she understood only about fifty percent of what he'd just said. Then Mr. Sheppard and Danny got into a long technical discussion about costs for shooting certain scenes and whether those scenes could be rewritten so they'd be cheaper to shoot. Neither of them looked in her direction or even motioned for her to take a seat, so she drifted back toward one of the white boards that were filled with writing, feeling rather idiotic.

Finally Danny glanced at his watch. "Okay, we'll summon the writers in ten for dinner. We're ordering from La Scala. Can we get you anything?" He looked from Mr. Sheppard to Anna.

She was about to decline when her boss said to bring them both pasta with mussels. "If you're a hit," he told Danny, "next year we'll squeeze enough money out of those sons of bitches to cover dinner and lunch. Anna, I need to go over a few things with Mason. Danny, give

Anna the new pages. When the food comes, call me."
Without saying goodbye, he walked out.

Danny motioned Anna into a seat. "How do you
like your internship?"

"It's my first day, so I actually don't know yet,"
Anna admitted, grateful to be off her feet. "And hon-
estly, I hardly know anything about TV."

"That won't last. Try not to let Clark intimidate
you—it's one of his specialties."

"I'll keep that in mind," Anna said dryly. "But I'm
not all that easily intimidated."

Danny nodded. "Good for you."

Anna cocked her head at him. "If you don't mind
my asking . . . I know he called you a 'boy wonder,' but
you do look really young to be the—what was it—
co–exec producer."

Danny leaned close. "I'm twenty-three, but don't let
it get around. I try to pass for twenty-eight." He
shrugged. "I just got lucky early. Right out of UCLA, I
wrote a spec *Buffy* that—"

A chubby, bespectacled girl with a pencil stuck
inside her messy bun and a clipboard in hand ran into
the conference room. "Hey, sorry to interrupt, Danny,"
she began. "But Pegasus is tweaking the dialogue with
Chyme in the next scene. She says her character would
never say the things we've got her saying."

Danny rolled his eyes as the girl pushed her clipboard at him. He took it and scanned it quickly.
"What's so complicated? Chyme tries to befriend her

and invites her to play tennis; Alexandra says something about not wanting to mess up her nails." He flipped to the next page. "Cruise shows up and Alexandra comes on to him."

Anna watched as the chubby girl shrugged. "Hey, I'm a lowly PA. She's not about to tell me. But she's yelling at Mason and he said that you have to fix it. Now. And please don't kill the messenger." She waggled her fingers at them and walked out.

"Shit. I knew they shouldn't have cast her," Danny muttered.

"The brunette in the lobby?" Anna asked.

Danny nodded. "She's supposed to be this rich-ass preppy girl. You know any girls like that?"

"I suppose I *am* a girl like that," Anna confessed. "And I couldn't help noticing—please tell me to shut up if I'm out of line . . ."

"No, go ahead, really," Danny urged her.

"Well, her nails. And the way she's dressed. New York prep school girls don't have red fingernails. And they don't wear Versace."

"Come on," Danny guffawed.

"I'm serious," Anna insisted. "I realize I'm speaking in generalities but . . . short nails, no polish. Not even French manicures—prep school girls like to pretend they don't care about things like that. And the Versace . . ." Anna shook her head.

"Wrong, huh?"

"An East Side prep school girl in New York would

wear something vintage, maybe. She could have found it in a thrift shop for five bucks. It could have holes in it. It looks like you don't care."

"But Alexandra—this character—her father is a billionaire. She comes from five generations of money."

So do I, Anna thought, but wasn't about to say so.

"Even more reason for her not to wear it on her back. Unless it's, say, vintage Chanel. Or she's being ironic, or—" Anna stopped herself and bit her lower lip. "God. I'm sorry. I shouldn't be telling you—"

"No, no, it's fine," Danny insisted. "I asked. And I think I just got an inkling of why Clark glommed onto you. I'll let the costume people know about it later. And hair and makeup."

Anna was flattered. "Thanks."

"You're welcome. Be right back. No, come watch this."

Anna followed Danny into the hallway, where a two-foot-high Chinese gong rested atop some filing cabinets. "You want to do the honors?" Danny asked. When Anna shook her head, Danny picked up a mallet and smacked the gong. The reverb filled the hallway.

"Low tech," Danny joked. "They'll be pissed. No time to work on their specs."

Summoned by the gong, the writers drifted back into the room. Some different production assistants came in and took dinner orders, which for some reason was a very big deal, with a lot of planning and menu consultation. Clark hadn't returned, so Anna sat apart from the group, feeling self-conscious all over again. But just as the assistants were finally departing, Danny leaned his chair back and whispered to her, "Hope you can hang out. We'll wrap up late, but we're going to hit Dublin's later; you should come with."

Anna had no idea what Dublin's was, but she was flattered by the invitation. As she sat there for the next hour listening to Danny Bluestone run the room, she grew more and more impressed with his talent and personality. Plus he was so cute in an offbeat, non-Hollywood kind of way.

Maybe she'd just take him up on his offer.

"It's nice. But I like your jacket better," Mia said, a bit petulantly. She stood in front of the mirror in Cammie's room in her new Moschino Cheap & Chic crepe blazer; black, with pink and yellow piping and buttons. Mia had wondered aloud why the clothing line was called "Cheap & Chic" when the jacket cost over a thousand dollars. Cammie explained that by their standards, that *was* cheap.

Cammie's new Champagne Jones metallic brocade, mink-lined clutch jacket had cost more than twice that, which had everything to do with why Mia wanted it.

"No bitching from you," Cammie ordered, slipping out of her heels to stretch her insoles on the plush carpet. Why did it have to hurt so much to wear expensive shoes? "Thanks to my dad's credit card, you now own a jacket that is worth more than your entire ratty valley girl wardrobe paid for by your mother."

Cammie had taken Mia to the Fred Segal in Santa Monica, the favorite shopping site of (a) the rich and famous, (b) the pretending to be rich and famous, and (c) the desperate to rub elbows with the rich and famous. She didn't like Fred Segal that much—the combination of the drive to Santa Monica and the gawking tourists was almost enough to make Cammie turn to a personal shopper when she wanted something from that store. Not today, though. She knew from experience that the acquisition of crafted fabrics—new clothing—would be far better for her wounded psyche than dozens of hours of psychotherapy.

After Fred Segal they drove back toward West Hollywood, where they trolled Melrose Avenue and stocked up on cute beaded T-shirts that went for eighty dollars a pop. These were so inexpensive that Cammie bought them in every color for herself and for Mia. Price wasn't much of an object: her father's accountant paid off the credit card bills every month in their entirety. She'd never heard a word about what she bought or how much it had cost.

The last stop on their excursion had been the Spanish Kitchen for dinner. Mia was practically hyperventilating to be taken there since she'd read in one of her teen rags that Jennifer and Brad were regular customers. Through their brief dinner movie stars and rumors about movie stars were the younger girl's sole topic of conversation.

For a while Cammie amused herself with shameless name-dropping, ninety-nine percent of it true. Cammie had been at Sarah Michelle's birthday party. She'd partied with Lenny Kravitz, pre-Nicole. She'd flown to New York with Sam and Dee in Jackson Sharpe's jet for Fashion Week and had front-row seats at Baby Phat and Imitation of Christ.

Mia hung on every word. In a way, it was fun to be with someone who was actually impressed with a life that Cammie took for granted. But the moment that Cammie tried to shift the conversation around to Mia, or why Mia was living with relatives in the valley instead of with her mother, or why her mother hadn't even mentioned a daughter until just a few days ago, Mia either dodged the question or changed the subject.

Not that Cammie cared. It was just that without more info on the newest family member, she couldn't leverage that information to her own benefit.

"Can I try on your jacket at least?" Mia asked.

"No." Cammie disappeared into her palatial bathroom, with its pale pink sunken Jacuzzi tub, separate stall shower with twelve jets at various levels, and antique French bidet. She used the facilities, then shed her clothes, dropping them wherever. She grabbed her hot pink velvet Aubade robe and shrugged into it, then padded back into the bedroom.

Mia stood in front of Cammie's mirror, wearing Cammie's new jacket.

Cammie's hands went to her narrow hips. "What did I tell you?"

"I'm not *contaminating* it, okay?"

"Take it off."

"Jeez, hold on, I'm just—"

"I said take it off!" Cammie thundered. This had been such a miserable day. That she had begun to plan her own eighteenth birthday party because no one else had thought to do it made her blood boil. Of course, Mia didn't know about that. But this girl was just one more example of how Cammie's nearest and dearest didn't consider her or her feelings at all.

Mia shook hair out of her eyes and started to take off the jacket. "Okay. I'm sorry."

For chrissake. What was taking her so long? Cammie reached for the free sleeve of the jacket to yank it off the younger girl. A sickening ripping sound filled the air as the sleeve detached.

"Look what you did!" Mia cried.

"What *I* did?"

Mia slipped off the rest of the jacket and threw it on the bed. "It's not my fault, you know. Besides, for what you spent, the jacket should be made better, don't you think?" Mia picked up her shopping bag and headed swiftly for the door, where she spun back to Cammie. She looked less than certain. "The store will take it back, right?"

Cammie sat down on her bed and shook her head, though there was every chance that it would. Let the girl sweat.

"Cammie?" Mia's voice was soft and tentative. "I just want to say that—"

"Hey, what's up, girls?" came Clark Sheppard's booming voice.

"Dad, hi! You're home early!" Cammie said brightly, bouncing up as her father stepped into her room.

It wasn't much after eight o'clock. Her father didn't usually show up until hours later. "Patrice and I have a charity thing to go to tonight," he explained, then took in the shopping bags arrayed on the floor. "You two hit the stores?"

"Cammie took me," Mia said. "It was really nice of her."

"Great." Clark beamed at Cammie. "Glad to see that you two are getting along better." He disappeared down the hall. Mia followed him.

Cammie sat again. This could not be happening. Her life could not be this out of control. She spied the small framed photo of her mother that she kept on her bedside and thought that if she were still alive, she'd certainly be planning a great eighteenth birthday party for her daughter. She picked up the photo and looked at it closely; it had been taken at her sixth birthday party. Her mother had her arm around Cammie's narrow shoulders. They wore matching dresses and matching smiles. But now Cammie was about to turn eighteen; such an important birthday, with no mom at her side, and the memories of her that she did have ebbed with each passing year.

A tear rolled down Cammie's cheek; she fisted it away. God, look what she'd come to, sitting alone in her room crying about her life. No fucking way. She was a gorgeous Hollywood princess. She'd simply throw herself a gorgeous Hollywood birthday party. She'd get Dee to help her; one shared Kabbalah class and she'd have the girl eating out of her hand again. And she'd definitely invite Sam and Adam. If they were a couple, she'd flirt with him outrageously to teach Sam a lesson.

And then, to show her who was boss, maybe she'd even invite Anna Percy.

Well, maybe not.

Spy

Dublin's was a rowdy Irish bar on the Strand in the town of Hermosa Beach, just a short walk to the actual beach. It served only beer, ale, and whiskey from Ireland and featured massive bowls of peanuts on every table. Customers shelled them and threw the shells onto the sawdust-covered floor. A huge dartboard in the back of the place featured Prince Charles as the bull's-eye. In another corner an old-fashioned jukebox blared vintage rock.

Anna sat next to Danny Bluestone at a long table of people who worked on *Hermosa Beach.* They were a boisterous group, going on and on about—what else— their show, other shows, other shows they had worked on, and who was the biggest son of a bitch in the business. Though Clark had departed the production offices after dinner, Anna had opted to stay and Clark had encouraged her to do so. He told her to listen, listen, and listen some more and report back to him. When she needed a ride home, she should call a certain limo service and bill it to Apex.

So for quite a while she'd stood out of camera range and watched some of the show actually being shot. She was surprised at how the dialogue was cut into such small chunks, then the director would call, "Cut," and the actors would wander off or get their makeup redone or change outfits while the next shot was set up. The process was rather dull, to tell the truth.

Clark had left Anna with a shooting script. Scenes were marked in the order in which they'd be shot, which wasn't the order of the scenes in the script. In the episode currently filming there were three scenes in the hotel lobby: one at the beginning of the show, one near the middle, and one at the end. All three scenes were shot back-to-back. The actors had to change costumes, but evidently that was easier and cheaper than shooting the show in chronological order.

As Anna looked down the table, she noticed there was a definite pecking order to the seating. The actors were sitting together. The guy who played Cruise looked a little like Ben but was darker and not as tall. Ben. She realized she'd barely thought of him all afternoon.

The waitress set four pitchers of ale on the long table. Danny reached for Anna's glass and filled it. "This is going to be the best ale you've ever tasted," he assured her.

Anna had no reason to argue since the truth was she'd never tasted any kind of ale before. She took a small sip through the foam. It tasted like urine, or what she imagined urine would taste like were she actually to drink it. She'd read about certain African tribes who drank their own as a curative for—

"What's the verdict?" Danny asked, taking a long pull.

"Interesting," Anna replied, trying to sound upbeat.

Danny threw his head back, laughing. "'Interesting?' The kiss of death. When an exec says that a certain plot point is interesting, you know you're about to get a new asshole. You hate it."

Anna nodded. "Sorry."

"Well, I promise not to make you chug. But I do propose a toast." Danny lifted his glass, so she did, too. "Here's to the new eyes and ears of Clark Sheppard, and what a major improvement over Clark's they are." He clinked his glass against hers.

Anna took the smallest of sips. "You make it sound like I'm Clark's spy."

"You are."

"No, I'm not," Anna protested. "I would never . . . That's ridiculous."

"Don't be offended. The guy's the biggest son of a bitch in show business. One time a director's mother died in the middle of a shoot. When the director took time off to go to the funeral, Clark fired him."

"You're kidding."

"I wasn't there. But that's what I heard." Danny took off his New York Yankees baseball cap and plopped it playfully on Anna's head. "Anyway, the notes you gave me on Alexandra were really helpful, you know." He cocked his head at her and grinned. "That cap never looked so good."

Anna tipped the hat lower on her forehead. "So, Danny. Do you like writing for TV?"

"I like the money," he answered. "I drive nice cars. I go on nice vacations. I send my younger brother nice presents for Hanukkah. But actually I'm writing a spec in my copious free time."

"Spec?" Anna echoed.

"A film no one is paying you to write," Danny translated, "after which your agent tries to sell it. It's tough, though. I work on *Hermosa Beach* six days a week in a good week—often until nine, ten at night. And I've been at it since early June."

"What's your movie about?"

"A man in pain searching for something to believe in," Danny quipped.

Anna nodded, trying to look solemn. "Ah, man against himself. How archetypal."

"I can't even spell *archetypal.* Anyway, college guy hitches around the country, then around the world, yadda, yadda. College guy ends up in the Peace Corps. No one will make it. Not sexy enough. But dumb me, it's the story I want to tell."

Anna was touched. "Well, if it's the story you want to tell, then it's not dumb."

He stared into his ale as if it was an oracle. "Truth is, it would make a better novel than a movie. That's what I'd really like to do: chuck all this, go live in a garret in

Paris, and write it. Am I a cliché or what?" He sipped his ale. "What about you, Anna?"

She shrugged. "Finishing high school, starting at Yale next fall."

Danny almost spat his ale. "You're still in *high school?*"

"Unfortunately."

"I thought for sure you were a college intern. Wow." He shook his head. "You don't seem like you're in high school."

"I'll take that as a compliment."

"Hey, you!" The actress who played Alexandra— Pegasus Patton—slid into a chair next to Anna that had just been vacated by one of the production assistants. She waved her hand in Anna's face. Her nails were no longer long and vermilion. Now they were short with no polish. "Are you responsible for this?"

"Not directly," Anna hedged.

"Bullshit." The girl leaned closer and blew boozy breath on Anna's face. "You're Clark's spy, right? They told me Clark's spy was some trust fund princess from the Upper East Side."

"I am not Clark Sheppard's spy," Anna insisted all over again. "I'm his *intern.*"

She waved a dismissive hand. "I do not appreciate having my character fucked with by some little intern, understandez-vous?"

"Allez vous faire enculer, et vite, s'il vous plaît," Anna said in an apologetic tone, with an impeccable Parisian accent. Which roughly and politely translated to: *Go*

have sex with yourself, and quickly, please, something that Anna would never have said in English but that in French sounded fabulous and not very obscene at all.

"Yeah, I like it that way, too," the actress agreed, pretending she understood what Anna had said. She got up and wove away.

"What'd you tell her?" Danny asked.

"Danny. When you go to Paris to write the great American novel, how are you going to cope if you can't speak the language?" Anna teased.

"I don't know. Maybe you'll be there to translate for me."

Anna smiled mysteriously and tried another sip of her ale. It seemed a bit less pissy. "Blue Suede Shoes" came on the jukebox—the Carl Perkins original version. Anna didn't know it, but she liked the beat. Some people down at the other end of the table got up to dance.

Danny watched the dancers for a moment. "Don't suppose you know how to jitterbug, Anna?"

"Actually, at finishing school one summer we learned everything from how to curtsy properly to every kind of interaction that might involve music." To illustrate, Anna held her arms up as if ballroom dancing.

"Finishing school?"

Anna nodded gravely. "Sure."

"We who?"

"Upper East Side trust fund princesses. What about you? Where'd you learn?"

"Living room. My mom." Danny took Anna's hand.
Together they headed for Dublin's small dance floor. As
Anna walked away, she could hear her cell phone ring in
her purse. She knew she should answer it. But really, all
she wanted to do was live in the moment, have fun, and
jitterbug with Danny.

Everything and everyone else could just wait. Even
Ben.

Hetero and Breathing

"That's all right, that's okay, you'll be working for us someday!"

Approximately twenty miles north of Hermosa Beach—at the same time that Anna was jitterbugging with Danny—the fans of Beverly Hills High's basketball team were chanting fervently, having slummed it north on the crowded 405 freeway to root against the home team of Birmingham High School in Van Nuys.

Van Nuys. Meaning area code 818. Meaning *the valley*. Meaning the San Fernando Valley, the vast flat suburban wasteland directly over the big hills that fortunately walled it off it from real places like Beverly Hills and Brentwood and Santa Monica. The valley was fifty square miles of boredom, always twenty degrees hotter or ten degrees colder than the rest of Los Angeles. The pollution was insufferable, the restaurants detestable, the clubs passé before they even opened. Los Angeles was famous for Beverly Hills and Hollywood. The valley was famous for its pornography industry.

As for Van Nuys, it skidded dangerously between lower-middle and middle class—the students on the home court side of the gym reflected these demographics. When Cammie gazed across the basketball court toward their fans, her eyes met an array of fashion disasters. Plus the Van Nuys girls were so fat! Yet even the fat ones were in skintight jeans and heels—like they were proud—and dipping talon-length fingernails into paper plates full of greasy nachos.

So gross.

Sam had invited Cammie to come to the game with her, saying that they hadn't seen each other much during the week. That was true, and that was the only reason Cammie deigned to sit on a hard bleacher seat in a high school she'd vowed never to set foot in, watching tall boys in baggy shorts attempt to throw an orange ball through a cord net. She hadn't hung out with Sam in a couple of days. Though she was loath to admit it, she missed Sam. And she thought she might be able to steer the conversation around to her birthday party and make Sam feel guilty as hell.

"That's all right, that's okay, you'll be working for us someday!"

The BHH chant went up again, provoking boos from the Van Nuys fans. Cammie half worried that one of the Van Nuys gangbangers would pull out a nine-millimeter Glock and start firing. Then she realized that was what the metal detectors at the doors were supposed to prevent.

"Thanks for coming on this excursion," Sam told

Cammie. "When was the last time you were over here in the valley?"

Cammie thought for a moment. "Never. I'm allergic."

Sam laughed. "It isn't that bad."

"Yuh, Sam, it is. Why are you here, anyway? I didn't know you were a basketball fan."

Sam flushed for a millisecond, which made Cammie very suspicious.

"What?" Cammie continued. "Is there a guy on the team you want to take home from the game?"

"No!" Sam retorted.

Cammie smiled. That "no" had come too quickly. She wasn't Clark Sheppard's daughter for nothing: sometimes "no" meant "maybe," and "maybe" meant "yes." And sometimes "no" definitely meant "yes." Like now.

But cheers from the Van Nuys side obliterated whatever Cammie was planning to say—the Van Nuys center had just sunk a free throw to put his team ahead by two points. There were less than ten seconds left to go in the fourth quarter, and Beverly Hills was clearly heading for defeat. But the hundreds of students and fans who had driven their Beemers, Masaratis, and Z Roadsters over the hill for this experience weren't deterred. Most of them had an ulterior motive for coming to the game: the post-game party.

Before Beverly Hills could inbound the ball under their own basket, Adam signaled the referee for a time-out so the team could talk things over. Cammie, fist under her chin, watched them. Adam Flood looked surprisingly good in baggy satin shorts. He had great definition in his upper arms, too. He was quite cute, albeit in a Midwestern hick sort of way.

"Hey, you guys!" Dee headed toward them, her Brooklyn guitar player, Stevie, in tow. "Sorry we're late." She plopped down next to Cammie.

Stevie sat next to her. "We were otherwise detained." He smirked.

Dee beamed at him. He leaned in and kissed her. Hard. Dee kissed him back. Their hands were all over each other.

"Kids, if you wanted seconds, you should have stayed on at the hotel," Cammie said sweetly. "There's only ten seconds left."

"We'll head back later," Stevie said, his hand squeezing Dee's thigh.

Well, well, well, Cammie thought. Look at our little Dee. Perhaps she'd finally ended her skein of falling for guys who always turned out to be gay. Or not.

The horn sounded to end the time-out, and the two teams filed back onto the court. The Van Nuys cheerleading squad yelled and hollered for their team. Cammie laughed. Their girls looked so ridiculous. At BHH, cheerleading was somewhere in the same social stratum as swine raising.

"Come on, Adam!" Sam shouted anyway, getting into it.

Dee stood up and pumped the air. "Woo-hoo! Go, Adam!"

God. School spirit. It was enough to make Cammie reach for her dark glasses and pretend she didn't know them.

The game restarted. A Beverly Hills player inbounded the pass to Adam, who dribbled three times and then fired a bounce pass to a forward in the right corner. Then Adam streaked across the court without the ball as the Van Nuys crowd counted down.

"FIVE! FOUR! THREE! TWO!"

At the two-second mark the forward heaved the ball back to Adam, who took it at the top of the key, just outside the three-point circle. He pump-faked . . .

"ONE!"

And let fly with a rainbow of a jump shot.

"Go in the basket!" Sam screamed as the buzzer sounded, ending the game.

The ball swished home. There was a huge roar from the Beverly Hills fans as Adam's teammates mobbed him. The Van Nuys fans, though, were stunned into silence, unable to believe that they'd just been beaten on a three-point basket launched only moments before time ran out. As the Van Nuys coach dashed onto the court to berate the impassive officials, Cammie almost smiled. It was too funny. People really cared about this shit.

Out on the court, Adam's grin was high voltage as he high-fived his teammates. Cute smile. In fact, the whole package was cute. But of course, he wasn't Cammie's type. The celebration wound down; Adam and his teammates ran back toward their dressing room, but not without acknowledging their cheering fans. Adam waved toward Cammie and Sam. Cammie watched Sam wave back. Big time. Which left Cammie with two big questions.

What was going on between them? And if there *was* something going on, why hadn't Sam talked to her about it?

The post-game party was at the home of Kyle Bauersachs, one of the substitutes on the Beverly Hills team. However, his father was the most successful personal injury lawyer in southern California, which was why the family owned one fantastic mansion off Bellagio Road in Bel Air and another oceanfront one in Malibu. Mr. and Mrs. Bauersachs permitted Kyle to host one post-game party per year, at the mansion of his choice.

Kyle had chosen Malibu this year. To ensure a good crowd at the Van Nuys game, he'd passed the word that any student who brought his or her ticket stub could come to the after party. Some enterprising kid had printed fake stubs and sold them for five bucks a pop, which accounted for why guys pushing a decade older than high-school were hitting on the high school girls. And why so many cars were trying to get over Topanga Canyon that there was a traffic jam at the turn onto Pacific Coast Highway.

Cammie somehow got separated from her friends soon after they came through the front door, so she strolled around on her own. The house was ultra-modern—in fact, it looked like it had been lifted wholesale from the set of *A Clockwork Orange.* All stark furniture, right angles, white walls, and vaguely phallic-looking sculptures, the main living room was a seething, writhing mass of students and friends celebrating the unlikely victory.

Cammie saw Kyle coming out of the kitchen, a case of Belgian beer in his arms. He was still in his basketball jersey, since he hadn't gotten into the game. His eyes lit up when he realized that Cammie Sheppard had actually showed up at his party. "Cammie! Hi!"

She waggled two fingers at him. "Nice party, Kyle."

"Hey, thanks. Catch me later, let's dance!"

She nodded, thinking, Over my cold, dead body, you loser.

She wandered into a game room, filled with pool tables, Foosball sets, and a giant plasma television that was showing music videos. To her left was a wide corridor that evidently led to a suite of bedrooms. A guy Cammie had never seen before leaned against the door frame and scanned her from head to foot and then back up again. At least twenty-five, and he already had a beer belly.

Ex–USC frat boy, Cammie thought automatically.

"What's your name, sweetheart?" The frat boy was saying hello.

"I don't have one," Cammie said, dripping vocal icicles. "When'd you graduate from the University of Southern California?"

"Two years ago," Frat Boy 25 said. "I'm Lenny.

Kyle's cousin. Mmm, you look good enough to eat. You been down to the hot tub, clothing *very* optional?"

"Gee, I haven't, Lenny. Not yet, anyway. You heading that way?"

"Oh yeah." Frat Boy 25 was practically drooling.

"Well, when you get there, Lenny, go fuck yourself. That is, if you can unearth any equipment below that gut of yours." Cammie pivoted and walked away, wondering why so many guys were such complete assholes and whether their mothers raised them to be that way.

Cammie toured the living room—wall-to-wall dancing—went out to the deck—drugs, drinks, and various stages of foreplay—and headed down to the beachfront patio—all of the above. But she was alone. Everyone seemed to be having a fabulous time but her. She slipped off her shoes and let them dangle from her fingers as she left the patio and walked through the lush sand all the way to the ocean's edge, where the raucous sound of the party mixed with the steady *whoosh-whoosh* of the incoming swells.

There she stood at the high-water line and stared morosely at the breakers. What was wrong with her lately? She just couldn't seem to get into a party mood. Even flirting was starting to feel like wasted energy.

Then Cammie saw movement in the moonlight about thirty yards down the beach. Adam Flood, in jeans and a sweatshirt. He was alone, too. Cammie watched as he skipped a flat stone against an incoming wave—the stone bounced five times before sinking into the water. Then he fished for something in his pocket, and Cammie heard the sound of a set of keys being extracted. Only then did he look up and see Cammie smiling at him.

"Leaving?" she asked. "You've come the wrong way. Valet's up by the Pacific Coast Highway."

Adam shrugged. "Don't seem to be in a party animal frame of mind."

"Me neither."

Adam laughed. "Color me shocked. I thought 'Party Animal' was Cammie Sheppard's middle name."

"Maybe you don't know me as well as you thought you did." Cammie's voice was almost a purr as she did an instant revise of her thought processes. Maybe flirting was fun after all. She fell in next to him, and they sauntered back toward the house. "You played a great game tonight."

He looked amused. "As compared to—?"

"What do you mean?"

"I mean, have you ever been to a basketball game before?"

"Not recently," Cammie admitted.

"Not ever," Adam corrected.

"If you want to be technical about it. But I had fun."

About halfway back to the house they reached an array of cushioned wooden benches that belonged to Kyle's family. Cammie sat and patted the seat next to her. But Adam rested on the next bench instead. He rubbed the back of his neck. "Man, I'm whipped."

She was about to offer to massage it for him, but something stopped her. "That last basket was fantastic."

"Thanks. You can't imagine how many times I've taken that shot in practice and missed." His smile crinkled the corners of his eyes. For the third time in twelve hours Cammie noticed how cute he was.

"Fifteen? Fifty?" Cammie asked, though she knew Adam's question was rhetorical. Then she remembered something that had been utterly unimportant in her life until this very instant. "You know, my dad has a skybox at the Staples Center. I'm sure he could hook you up if you wanted to see the Lakers sometime."

Cammie expected Adam to jump at the chance, but he didn't. "You know, I'd rather play on that court when no one else is around than be in the stands for game seven of the play-offs," Adam said softly. "Ghosts."

"Ghosts?"

"Yeah. If you listen hard enough. Magic, Jerry West, Kareem. Ghosts."

Cammie had lived in Los Angeles long enough to know that Adam was referring to Los Angeles Lakers greats of the past. "Well, if you ever change your mind . . ."

"Thanks." He stood but hesitated. "Did you want to go back in, or—?"

"Hang out with me a few more minutes, okay?" she pleaded. Then she took a shot in the dark. "I know you want to go find Sam, but . . . I thought we could talk."

He sat again, albeit reluctantly. And he didn't say

anything about Sam, which Cammie interpreted as a good sign. She stretched, showing off her diamond-and-ruby navel ring plus the gold belly chain that sat above the top of her jeans. She saw Adam notice it. How could he not? He was hetero and breathing, wasn't he?

"Can I ask you a question?"

"Shoot."

"Well, I know that you and Anna . . . that is, I heard how badly she treated you."

Adam shook his head. "I don't want to talk about that."

"I understand. It's just . . . Sam is my best friend," Cammie said, oozing sincerity. "And I really don't want to see her hurt."

"Sam? We're not . . . We're buds."

Interesting. Because Cammie had been convinced that Sam wanted a lot more from Adam than friendship. Well, it served Sam right for spending her time with that bitch Anna instead of with Cammie. Cammie would have figured out Adam's only-friendship vibe a long time ago and warned Sam that Adam wasn't into her.

Adam checked his watch. "Hey, I really have to go, Cammie."

"Never hurry, never worry." Cammie smiled, quoting her favorite childhood book, *Charlotte's Web.*

Adam grinned. "You're an E. B. White fan?"

"That book always reminds me of my mom," Cammie said, standing up and stretching luxuriantly. "Can I walk you back to the house?"

Adam stood, too. "Sure."

Out of the corner of her eye Cammie spotted Sam heading toward them. "But first," Cammie said, "there's something I've wanted to do ever since that final buzzer went off."

"Yeah?" Adam asked.

Making sure that she and Adam were positioned so that Sam had the best-possible sight line, Cammie wrapped her arms around Adam's neck. Then she gave him the softest, most promising of kisses. "Good job," she whispered in his ear.

"Uh . . . thanks," he said, edging slightly away from her.

Understandable. He'd probably never been hit on by a girl with as powerful a mojo as Cammie's. But the truly, deeply weird thing was, at that moment, her focus wasn't on showing Sam who was boss. She wasn't even thinking about how much Adam had to want her after that. Because the most bizarre thing had just happened: *she* was the one, not him, whose breath caught in her throat. Because all she wanted to do was to go on kissing Adam Flood.

Five Different Camera Angles

Anna twisted her key into the front door of her father's house and disarmed the alarm before it could send a silent alert to the Beverly Hills police department. Once the alarm was off, she slipped out of her black velvet Chanel ballet flats and dangled them on two fingers as she headed upstairs to her room. Before she undressed for the night, she remembered that she'd turned off her cell phone at Dublin's, so she powered it back up. It hadn't been activated for thirty seconds before it chimed.

"Hello?"

"Anna? Are you okay?" Ben. Sounding panicked.

"Yes, I'm fine," she assured him.

"I called you four times," Ben said. "Once you didn't answer, the other times your phone was off. You scared the piss out of me."

"I was working," Anna said as she sat on her bed. "Clark Sheppard took me to the set of *Hermosa Beach*."

"And kept you until midnight?" Ben asked. "What a schmuck."

"I'm sorry I didn't pick up your calls." She wondered what she should tell Ben about Danny Bluestone. If anything.

"As long as you're all right. So, listen. Didn't you mention that tomorrow was some kind of city education conference, so there's no school?"

She had.

"So I thought we could spend the day together. Maybe head down to the South Bay beaches or up to Carpinteria—the weather's supposed to be great. And then tomorrow night we can have dinner at my house. My parents want to meet you. If you can deal, that is. So, you up for it?"

"Sure," Anna said. Ben's idea really did sound like fun, except perhaps for the dinner-with-the-parents part. But she couldn't very well tell her boyfriend that she didn't want to meet his folks. And Clark hadn't said anything to her about having to work that day.

"Great. I'll pick you up early, say nine?"

She agreed, they said good night, and then Anna hung up. For a moment she sat on her bed, staring at nothing, convincing herself that she really *did* want to spend the day with Ben. It would be fantastic. All those romantic feelings for him would still be there. She was sure of it.

She picked up her messages. Ben. Ben *again*. And then her father, calling from Arizona.

"Hey, sorry I missed you. I just wanted to tell you that your sister's doing fine at White Mountains. She actually hugged me before I left—that's gotta be some kind of progress. I spoke with one of the counselors there, who's pretty optimistic. So listen, I've decided to take a few more days off, maybe a week. Thought I'd drive over to Taos in New Mexico and get in some skiing. Thought you might want to join me. Call my cell and let me know. Hope you're not too lonely rattling around in that house. Make sure Django takes care of whatever you need, honey. Ciao."

He clicked off. So did Anna. She pulled off her clothes and padded into the bathroom to shower, thinking that it was typical of her father to suggest that she join him, as if school and other commitments simply didn't exist.

After her shower she slipped into the antique lace nightgown her grandmother had given her on her last birthday, got into bed, and turned out the light. Moonlight streamed in through the window; arched lines of light and dark played over her paisley quilt. She lay there, gazing at them, wondering at her own behavior.

Beware of what you wish for.

Anna had wished for Ben. Her wish had come true. Yet only a few days later she'd found herself with Danny, as if she didn't have a boyfriend at all. And what about Django? She liked him. A lot.

Anna knew what her best friend in Manhattan, Cyn, would say. Cyn would tell her in that all-knowing way she had that flirting meant she wasn't ready to be tied down. But what if it simply meant Anna was fickle? Or that she was afraid of a real relationship? The last thing she wanted was to be like Cammie Sheppard, who reveled in flexing her sex appeal simply because she could. It was so . . . so . . . tawdry.

No. That wasn't her.

So what, then? She snuggled under the covers and closed her eyes. Her final thought before falling asleep was this: What if it meant that she really did want a relationship . . . but she had simply picked the wrong guy?

All Anna's fears of the night vanished with the morning sun. Ben picked her up at nine on the dot; he looked hot in simple khaki shorts and a white tee. It had been Ben's idea that they drive down to Hermosa Beach but hers to offer a tour of the TV show set later in the day. So what if she had enjoyed a mild flirtation with Danny the night before? She was in a relationship, yes, but she wasn't dead. That Ben declined her offer didn't bother her at all.

They breakfasted at Two Hussies, a restaurant on the corner of the Strand, the broad pedestrians-only strip of restaurants and boutiques that met the asphalt walk by the beach. It was unusually warm for January, and they were able to sit outside, overlooking the sand and surf. Ben sat next to her so that they both faced the ocean, an arm draped loosely around her shoulders. A steady stream of runners, joggers, and Rollerbladers passed them on the walkway, either heading north toward Santa Monica or south toward Palos Verdes. The asphalt, Ben told her, stretched for seventeen miles.

"Man, this is the life," he said with a sigh. "I read in the *Times* today that the high in New York yesterday was three degrees. Fahrenheit. Hard to believe."

She leaned into him. "Does it make you wish you weren't going back?"

He grinned at her. "*You* make me wish I wasn't going back."

Their waitress, clad in a skintight abbreviated Hussy logo shirt and short-shorts that looked spray-painted to her thighs, brought their breakfast: eggs Benedict for him, a veggie omelet for her. The waitress refilled their coffee, offered a perfunctory smile, and headed back inside. Anna checked to see if Ben's eyes followed her retreating butt. They didn't, so she repositioned her napkin on her lap, uncomfortable that she was testing him like that.

"This is so different from the East Coast," she mused, trying to make conversation.

"How's that?" Ben asked as he cut into his eggs.

Anna took a sip of coffee. "We had a house in the Hamptons for years. East. God, I loved it. An old colonial, right on the beach, on a street that looked as if you'd gone back in time," she remembered. "My mother sold it when Susan started high school—she never said why. Susan and I were ready to go back, like we did every summer, and she casually dropped that she'd sold it, just like that. After that, we'd stay there with friends, but it was never the same."

"So how was it different than this?" Ben asked.

Anna toyed with a slice of omelet. "Oh, it's all snotty wealth and good breeding—or people trying to pass as that," she said with a laugh. "One year a good friend of my mother's had a show at *Downtown Guild Hall*. Of course, she insisted that Susan and I dress up in little Lilly Pulitzer outfits, and—"

"Whoa, back up. What kind of show *where?*"

"An art show. Modern art. But it was really Susan and I who were on display. 'Cross your ankles when you sit, girls. Don't muss your dresses, girls.'"

Ben shook his head. "What about beaches and sand castles and playing with dead crabs?"

"We did all that," Anna agreed. "But everything is so much more formal than this. They do their best to keep the riffraff out. It's difficult to describe."

Ben hooked his pinkie to hers. "Well, we'll just have to go back there together. Who knows? Maybe one day we can buy your old house."

She smiled because it was such a sweet notion. "Or maybe I'll visit you at Princeton in the spring and take you to Montauk Point. It really is spectacular."

Ben put his fork down. "Can you lighten up on the Princeton talk?"

Why was he so irked? It didn't make any sense to her. Unless . . . yes. That had to be it.

"Are you worried about your parents being able to afford it?"

"Afford what?"

"Princeton. Tuition."

"It's complicated."

Anna shrugged. "That's okay. I'll listen."

"It's not money," Ben told her earnestly. "It's just that I'm still worried about my mom and dad. Dad's going to Gamblers Anonymous meetings. And Mom's doing okay. But still."

"I understand. But you were the one who told me that we have to stop trying to be the ones to fix our families. That it wasn't our responsibility." She bit off a piece of her omelet and chewed it thoughtfully.

"I did." Ben smiled. "Sometimes it's easier if you don't practice what you preach—if your head tells you one thing and your heart tells you another. Anyway, I have it all worked out with Princeton. If I get back there at a reasonable time and do okay on my midterms, there'll be no problems."

"Sure?" Anna asked.

"Sure." Ben balled up his napkin and threw it on the table. "Nah. Enough of this serious East Coast crap. I'm a California boy, and you, my dear, are now an honorary California girl. So what do you say we do something totally West Coast?"

"Get wasted and have sex on the beach?" she teased.

"Hell, yeah!" Ben threw his head back, laughing. He saw the waitress out of the corner of his eye and motioned for the check. "But first, let's get out there."

"Out where?" Anna asked.

Ben smiled. "Trust me."

Get out there, Anna learned, was California's unofficial slogan. And from Ben's point of view, it meant not sitting around like a spectator, but participating in the incredible range of outdoor activities that made southern California such a paradise spot. Which was why, by the time the sun was low in the afternoon sky, Anna and Ben were happy, tired, and more than a little disheveled.

They'd joined a pickup volleyball game. Walked along the ocean's edge and watched a couple of surf casters pull huge ocean perch from the water, one after another after another. Rented bicycles and ridden south toward Redondo Beach. And then, for the pièce de résistance, Ben had booked them on a boat ride that took them from Redondo all the way out to Santa Barbara Island. There a certified naturalist had guided them in a sea kayak along the rocky shoreline, to the chiding but harmless consternation of hundreds of barking seals and sea lions that called the island their home.

It was, Anna thought, as she and Ben pedaled back from Redondo Beach to Hermosa Beach, one of the best days she'd had since she'd come to California. And maybe one of the best days ever.

But just as the Hermosa Beach pier was coming into view, Anna's cell phone rang. She stopped her bicycle to answer it. "Hello?"

"I need you to pick up some dailies." It was Clark Sheppard, with no preliminaries and all the manners of an ill-tempered *Homo erectus.* "How soon can you get to the set?"

"How far are we from the Strand in Hermosa Beach?" Anna asked Ben.

"Five minutes," Ben told her. Anna reported this to Clark.

"Good." Clark hung up.

"What a lovely man," Anna said, putting her cell back in her purse.

"What's up?" Ben asked.

She quickly explained her mission. "Sorry," she added as they started off again. "I guess a day off from school doesn't mean a day off from interning."

But Ben was easy about the detour to the set and didn't even seem to mind that he'd have to give her an immediate ride to Westwood to deliver the dailies to Clark. Anna only knew what dailies were because Danny had mentioned them: they were raw videotapes of scenes from the show so that interested parties could see what was happening on the set. One "daily" might show one scene from five different camera angles, repeated in five different "takes."

Ben's guesstimate was accurate. Five minutes later they'd parked their bicycles and Anna was leading Ben through the hotel's spectacular lobby. No filming was in progress, so the set was deserted save for some designers refreshing the flowers with new ones that looked exactly like the old ones.

Anna found Danny in his small office, banging away on a keyboard. When he saw Anna, he gave her a "happy to see you" look and a little wave but then continued typing. Anna waited for a minute or two as Danny completed whatever he was working on, then came around his desk and enveloped her in a bear hug. "Hey, dancing partner! Great to see you!"

"You too," she said when he released her. "Danny Bluestone, Ben Birnbaum," she added, introducing the guys to each other. Danny held out a friendly hand, which, Anna could see, Ben shook with an iron grip.

"Danny's a writer on the show," Anna went on, choosing to ignore the scowl that had taken over her boyfriend's face. Ben didn't say a word, so she muttered something about picking up the dailies for Clark.

"Yeah, I just got his message," Danny said, reaching for a stack of tapes on his desk. He rearranged the rubber band around them, then gave them to Anna. "He could have just used a messenger service."

"I think he enjoys telling me what to do," Anna said ruefully. "Anyway, thanks."

"Not a problem." Danny sat on the edge of his desk. "Hey, come back later on—we're gonna hit Dublin's again. Nice to meet you, Ben."

Anna could feel Ben's ire as they left Danny's office, crossed the hotel lobby, and headed back outside. Truth be told, she felt awful. It had seemed like such a small deception when she'd let Ben think that she hadn't picked up his calls the night before because she was working.

"Um, you gonna explain that?" Ben finally asked when they reached their bicycles.

"The cast and crew went out last night and invited me along."

"You told me you were working."

Anna didn't reply.

"What's up with you and that guy?" Ben demanded.

"Nothing," Anna said quietly.

"That's a load of crap. If it was nothing, you wouldn't have lied to me about it."

"I didn't lie to you, exactly—"

"What the hell would you call it?"

"Would you calm down, please? You're making something out of nothing."

"Maybe." Ben started walking his bicycle down the path toward the shop where they'd rented them, and Anna pushed hers along, too.

"Maybe I didn't tell you because I thought you'd overreact, which is exactly what you're doing."

"Don't twist this around, Anna," Ben insisted.

"I just . . . I don't think we have to get so . . . so intense."

"That ice maiden shit might intimidate the hell out of guys back east, Anna, but it doesn't mean squat to me. Either we're together or we're not."

She touched his back with her free hand. "You know I want to be with you. But I have a life, too."

"Jeez, I can't even trust you when I'm in the same city. How am I supposed to trust you if I go back to Princeton?"

She knew he meant the question rhetorically. What

she couldn't quite figure out was how they'd gotten from being two people who wanted each other desperately to Ben feeling jealous—and her feeling guilty—if she so much as looked at another boy.

BAP Days

As Adam Flood pulled a vintage Public Image Limited T-shirt out of his top dresser drawer, a photograph he'd stuck on top of that dresser caught his eye. The photo was of him and Anna on the beach with his dog, Bowser. Adam had his arm around Anna, and the dog was gazing soulfully up at her.

Adam remembered the day that photo had been taken. He and Anna and the dog had been at the beach near Gladstone's, the famous seafood restaurant. Some Japanese tourists wandered by and asked Adam if he'd take their picture. Afterward they'd insisted on snapping one of him and Anna and the dog and had promised to mail it to him. Though Adam had scrawled his address on a scrap of paper, he'd never expected to see the photo. But it had arrived only a few days later, in an envelope from the Century City Plaza Hotel. Evidently the very honest tourists had developed their film before returning to the Land of the Rising Sun.

Anna and he hadn't been a couple then. They weren't a couple now. What Adam had never expected was that if there were a relationship, it would last roughly the same amount of time as a typical tourist's visit to Disneyland. Goddamn Ben. Adam should have known that Anna would run back to him. Girls always ran back to guys like Ben Birnbaum.

Morose, he sat on his bed. Bowser trotted into his room, and Adam absentmindedly stroked his dog's ears. Anna had told him she was ending their relationship to be alone for a while. What a crock. Then she'd had the nerve to pull that "I want us to be friends" line. He'd almost bought it, too.

With a final scratch to Bowser's fur, Adam sprang up and headed into his bathroom to brush his teeth. He wasn't pining for Anna, exactly. Nor was he in love with her. But he knew he'd been in the process of falling in love with her, deeply, truly, really in love. There was just something about her, something unlike any other girl he'd ever known and certainly unlike any other girl he'd known since moving from Michigan to Beverly Hills. For example, he liked Sam Sharpe. But her obvious insecurities gave her so much emotional baggage, he found it exhausting to hang out with her sometimes.

Then there was Cammie. It had shocked the hell out of him when she'd kissed him on the beach. And only a mannequin wouldn't have enjoyed that. But he knew her reputation—there was always an agenda with that one. Friends like Cammie made scorpions seem obsolete.

With new resolve, Adam strode back into his room

and took the photograph off his dresser. He tore it in two and dropped it in his wastebasket before heading downstairs.

"Rotten, Johnny," his mom said archly when she saw the T-shirt. She was at her desk in the family room, poring over some legal briefs. Both of Adam's parents were entertainment lawyers; they practiced together at the same firm. As far as Adam could see, that they continued to like and respect each other was a true Beverly Hills rarity.

Adam pulled on his ratty, ancient denim jacket. "So, I'm heading out."

His mom took off her reading glasses and frowned for a moment until she recalled his plans for the evening. "Beck. Hollywood Bowl. Right?"

He nodded.

"With?"

"Me. Solo."

"What about Anna?"

"There is no more Anna. He tried to shrug it off. "It's okay. I'm over her."

His mother nodded but didn't look convinced. "Have fun."

He held up the keys to her Saturn. "Thanks for this."

"You're welcome—put some gas in it," his mom said, putting her glasses back on.

Adam went outside, started her car, and slipped Beck's *Sea Change* CD into the player. It suited his mood more than the sexy undertones of *Midnite*

Vultures. Sea Change was all about bitter breakups and broken hearts—far more appropriate.

A half hour later he was part of the long line of cars snaking into the Bowl's parking lots, and then he felt as if he had to walk a mile through the greenery of Griffith Park before he reached the entrance to the outdoor concert space. He'd only been up to the Bowl once before, and that had been with his parents to see Sting. It had been his mom's birthday—she was the world's biggest Sting fan. He'd actually enjoyed the concert, except when his mom decided to sing along to "Roxanne" at the top of her lungs.

Adam had the best seat he could afford, which unfortunately meant nosebleed territory. He hadn't thought to bring binoculars, either. As the vast outdoor amphitheater filled, he took in the amazing architecture, the signature proscenium arch that he knew offered outstanding acoustics for an outdoor arena.

He settled down, waiting for the warm-up band to start. To his left were some high-school kids in Harvard-Westlake sweatshirts, to his right a couple of men in their twenties. But Adam didn't mind being at the concert alone; he knew he could easily have invited one of his buds from the basketball team. Or even Sam Sharpe. But it didn't seem fair to saddle anyone with his brood over life, love, and lust. Over Anna.

While Adam was waiting for the music to begin, Cammie paced the floor of her room, cell phone in hand.

As she waited for Sam to answer, she could hear strains of Christina Aguilera coming from Mia's room. God. The girl's taste in music was as bad as her taste in clothes.

Sam had promised that she'd call. In the olden BAP days—Before Anna Percy—a promise from Sam that she'd call meant that the phone would be ringing before noon. In the olden days Cammie would have already reminded Sam about Cammie's upcoming sweet eighteenth birthday, at which point Sam would have jumped in and offered to do anything to help plan the blowout to end all blowouts.

That was then, this was now. Night had fallen, and Sam still hadn't called her. So Cammie had figured out a plausible rationale for being the one to place the call. God forbid she should sound needy.

"Yuh?" Sam answered on the third ring. There was noise in the background, so Sam had to be out and about. Without Cammie. Something else that wouldn't have happened BAP.

"Hey, girl," Cammie greeted her. "What's up?" She stopped in front of her three-way mirror to check out her new Jolie silk bra and matching panties.

"Not much."

"Where are you?"

"Beauty Bar," Sam yelled over the club's noise.

Cammie knew the Beauty Bar, of course. Just off Hollywood Boulevard, it was done up exactly like a 1950s beauty salon and was one of the hip places of the moment. "Who's there?" Cammie tried to sound nonchalant.

"Dee was, but she left for Stevie's gig at the Hollywood Bowl. He's opening for Beck, isn't that cool?"

"Listen, about last night," Cammie went on smoothly. "I just wanted to check and make sure you were okay that Adam kissed me."

"You kissed him," Sam corrected her. "I saw. And it was just a peck anyway; it's not like it was leading to anything."

"Whatever."

Before she could figure out what to say next, Sam broke in. "You want to meet me at Johnny Rockets? I gotta get out of here. Three wanna-bes have already hit me up for roles in my new film."

Roles in her new film? Cammie thought. What a pretentious crock of shit. Just because Sam had announced in class that she and Anna were doing a new project didn't mean that anyone cared. Sometimes Sam's pitiful attempts to step out from her father's shadow were just so pathetic.

Instead of responding to Sam's question, Cammie asked, "Where's Adam?"

"Hollywood Bowl," Sam replied. "He's insane for Beck. Didn't you know?"

Of course Cammie didn't know. If she had, she would have told Adam that her father and Beck's manager were best friends. But it wasn't like Adam Flood confided in her.

"He didn't ask you to go with him?" Cammie queried.

"We're friends, that's all," Sam replied guilelessly. "I might be interested in him long term. But he's kind of on the rebound from Anna now. So I don't think he's really up for a relationship. You know what I mean?"

Cammie smiled. "That's frighteningly mature of you."

"I guess. We'll see what happens. Anyway, Adam knows, like, every lyric Beck ever wrote," Sam went on. "He's got a shitty seat, though. Nosebleed section. So, you want to meet for a burger?"

The hamsters in Cammie's mind started spinning their little metal wheels. Sam was backing off from Adam. Adam had gone to see Beck alone. He had a crap seat. She had the ability to make all his little I-love-Beck dreams come true. He'd be sooo grateful. This time he'd kiss her. And then she'd find out if what she thought she'd felt the night before was really something more than PMS cramps.

Suddenly Sam forgetting about her upcoming birthday had fallen off her list of priorities.

"I've got plans," Cammie said coolly. "Call me tomorrow."

Cammie leaned forward on the gray Italian leather seat to speak to her father's driver. "Pull up to 'will call.'"

It hadn't taken Cammie more than a half hour to set her plan in motion. One cell phone call to her father's assistant was all it took. ("My father needs two back-stage passes to Beck. And pronto.") Fifteen minutes later the passes were arranged, waiting at the box office. Meanwhile Cammie applied three coats of MAC mascara, brushed on some Nars blush in Orgasm, and finished with some baby pink Stila lip gloss. She decided to go with a casual look Adam was likely to appreciate—jeans she'd paid two hundred dollars for at the Beverly Center that were faded and patched to Woodstock-era vintage perfection, a wife-beater sleeveless man's T-shirt through which her red Jolie silk bra was plainly visible, and a vintage jean jacket. Yes, the jacket was lined in mink, and yes, it was conceivable that Adam was one of those PETA lunatics, but fuck it. A girl could only go so far to make herself over for a guy.

Outside the Hollywood Bowl box office the driver opened the door for Cammie; she hopped out. After issuing him instructions as to where he should wait, she went to will call for her backstage passes. With the laminated card dangling from her neck, she'd have the run of the place. Plus she'd arrived at the perfect time. Border Cross was just finishing their opening set, waving to the crowd before running from the stage. Dee's squeeze was wearing black leather pants. How excruciating was that? It could mean one of two things. Either Stevie Nova-whatever-his-name-was was gunning for the Harry Shearer role in a remake of *Spinal Tap* or Dee had fallen once again for a closeted gay boy.

While onstage a dozen roadies were doing a quick changeover for Beck, Cammie headed for the upper-tier section where she knew Adam was sitting. She herself had never been anywhere besides tenth row center at the Hollywood Bowl. It was almost like a foreign country up here, so far from the action. Why bother to come at all?

Okay. She was up top. Now how to find him?

Cammie decided to let him find her. She went down the first row of upper-tier seats and started to make her way across from left to right. If Adam was in his seat, he'd be sure to see her. He was such a polite guy that he'd call out to her. And if he was taking a bathroom break, she'd just repeat the process from right to left. She walked extra slowly and tossed around her red curls as much as possible. They were as bright and eye-catching as anything else Adam might notice.

"Cammie!"

Cammie hadn't moved more than thirty feet from where she started when she heard Adam's voice. That was even easier than expected.

Feigning surprise, she scanned the seats up above her. There was Adam, in the worst possible seat—second-to-last row from the top at the extreme right side. After an appropriately long moment she made eye contact with him and waved. Then she took her time making her way up to his row, half wishing that she had an oxygen mask. What was the point of going to a concert and sitting in a seat so far from the stage that the feature act looked like a paramecium?

"Hi there," she said. She slid into the temporarily unoccupied seat next to his.

"Cammie Sheppard. Will wonders never cease? The

serfs and the underlings sit up here. The pissant peas-
ants. The little people. Are you telling me that you were
hanging with the unwashed masses?"

She lifted his arm playfully and inspected it. Taut.
Tan. Nice.

"*Au contraire.* It appears that you do wash." She let
his arm go but rested her hand lightly on his forearm.
"Not everyone I know is rich. I don't judge people
based on money."

"But what are you doing all the way up here?"

Cammie thought quickly. "Dee said that Stevie's
cousin's girlfriend was in the upper tier. She asked me
to bring her a pass to the post-show party at the
Century City Plaza Hotel."

He didn't look convinced, so she playfully nudged
his shoulder with her own. "Oh, come on. Lighten up.
Sam mentioned you'd be here, so I thought I'd come
over and say hi. Who are you here with?"

"Came alone, actually."

"Really?" she purred, all innocent. "I'm with Dee,
but she's probably backstage worshiping at the shrine
of Stevie Novellino's leather pants by now while he pre-
tends that her name is Dick. Anyway, I'm a huge Beck
fan."

Adam showed the first sign of interest. "Yeah? Me
too. So what's your favorite?"

Shit. Cammie's brain went on overdrive. Beck. Beck.
Alt god of girls who don't wash their hair. No, wait.
Hadn't she overheard her dad talking to his manager

about some benefit thing for Willie Nelson? Well, it was worth a shot.

"I have to tell you . . . I do kind of like the country stuff," Cammie ventured. "But don't let it get around."

"No kidding?" Adam marveled, his eyes lighting up. "Me too! Did you hear him do Hank Williams's 'Lonesome Whistle'? So awesome."

Cammie nodded. "I totally agree."

"What else?" Adam asked eagerly.

Double shit. She'd have to pull an answer out of her butt. "The one he did at Farm Aid? You know. The one everyone loved . . ." She snapped her fingers like she was trying to remember.

"'Rowboat'?" Adam asked. "That's killer!" He seemed to be appraising her with new eyes. "So, Cammie Sheppard. You like Beck. Cool."

"More than cool." She casually exposed the laminated backstage pass that she'd tucked under the mink lining of her jacket.

Adam's eyebrows hit his hairline. "How'd you score that?"

"I told you, my dad and his manager have a professional relationship," Cammie said truthfully, and followed it with a hell of a whopper. "You see, I have Dee's pass, too. I guess Stevie got her in with his band." She extracted the extra pass from her jeans pocket. "Why don't we watch Beck from downstairs? Afterward I'll take you into his dressing room and introduce you."

"You're kidding."

"No, I'm not. . . ."

He held his palms up and grinned in a way that lit up his entire face. "I'm your man."

Oh, Adam, Cammie thought, you have no idea.

Watching Beck perform from orchestra-level, tenth-row center seats was fantastic enough. But going backstage to watch the two encores from the wings of the stage and then being a part of the post-show party at the Century City Plaza blew Adam away.

First of all, he and Cammie arrived at the famous elliptically shaped hotel by limo, which had been waiting for them right outside the gates to the Hollywood Bowl—Cammie assured Adam that they could easily return for his car later, when there wasn't a gargantuan traffic jam waiting to get out of the arena. He'd seen the wide-eyed, jealous stares from the guys and girls streaming past them to return to the parking lot—the girls jealous that they didn't have to fight the traffic, the guys jealous that he was with a girl as stunning as Cammie Sheppard.

At the hotel's semi-circular driveway, valets practically did battle for the right to open the doors to the limo. Once they were inside the expansive lobby, a representative from Beck's record label saw their backstage passes and corralled them—the post-show party was being held out back of the hotel, alongside the enormous heated swimming pool. The pool was closed to the general public for the night; a phalanx of security guards made sure that the riffraff was kept out and the beautiful people allowed in. But the magic backstage passes around their necks gave them easy access; within seconds they were inside the purple velvet ropes.

Adam felt Cammie slip one arm through his. "How about a drink?" she asked.

He spotted the open bar and a lavish buffet table at the far end of the pool. "Sure. What would you like?"

"Champagne. Join me?"

Adam shook his head. "Coach would kill me if he found out I was drinking champagne while I was in training."

Cammie threw her head back and laughed, her strawberry blond curls shaking seductively on her shoulders as she did. "Adam Flood, what do you think the chances are that your basketball coach is going to be at the after-show party for *Beck?*"

Now it was Adam's turn to laugh. He ordered orange juice to Cammie's Moët & Chandon and thought he saw a look of respect in Cammie's eyes when they clinked glasses.

"I thought there'd be a lot more people," he said, surveying the pool area. It wasn't empty, but it wasn't crowded, either. The atmosphere was, if anything, subdued.

"I've been to a lot of these; it depends on the musician. Kid Rock and P. Diddy's post parties were pretty raucous. But sometimes it's just a bunch of people up in a hotel suite doing drugs and—"

"Cammie! Cammie Sheppard!"

Adam and Cammie turned in the direction of a moon-faced guy in his thirties, wearing a Funk Daddy baseball cap, who was hustling in their direction.

"Who the hell is he?" Cammie murmured. As for Adam, the moon-faced guy looked somewhat familiar, but he couldn't remember where he'd seen him before.

The guy answered Cammie's question quickly enough. "Rick Resnick! From Jackson Sharpe's wedding!" He pulled Cammie into an unwilling embrace.

Now Adam remembered. At the New Year's Eve wedding of Sam's father and Poppy Sinclair, Rick had been one of the guests. He was a record producer; he and Dee's father were friends. And he had totally humiliated Anna.

Anna. Couldn't he stop thinking about her? And couldn't the world stop sending people his way that made him think about her?

A few other people drifted over to join the conversation—Dee Young and her father, among others. The conversation quickly turned to other post-show parties that they'd attended and how the buffet and open bar at this one compared to those. Adam had zero interest, so he told Cammie that he needed to use the facilities, which was true enough. He drifted back toward the hotel, skirting clumps of music industry types who stood together in clusters, talking.

Just as he neared the velvet ropes, though, he heard something unusual: the faint but very pleasant notes of an acoustic guitar being plucked. Curious, he followed the music across a grassy lawn to his right. As he got closer, he realized that what had sounded like a single guitar was actually two. Then at the far end of the lawn, on a pair of white plastic chairs nestled between three palm trees, he spotted the source. Two men were picking together, heads bowed so that they were almost touching. One had extremely long gray hair and a red bandanna.

Willie Nelson, who Adam hadn't even realized was at the party. And with him Beck himself.

Their fingers flew furiously, picking out the notes of a rollicking bluegrass tune. Adam froze, not wanting to disturb them. That was when Willie Nelson looked up, saw him, and smiled. Then with a cock of his head, he indicated that Adam should join them if he wanted to.

Adam—heart pounding at his good fortune—had to stop and pull himself together. Then he gave a little wave and practically floated to an empty chair. There he sat down, grinning from ear to ear, listening to two of his musical heroes jam.

An hour later he was still there, sure that if he wasn't in heaven, he was close.

Oops

Ben's house was cedar shingled like a New Mexico country cottage, only in this case the "cottage" was at the top of tony Stone Canyon Drive in Bel Air and covered seven thousand square feet. Anna was there for dinner with the Birnbaums. Ben had offered to pick Anna up, but she'd told him that she'd drive over herself. Now, as she turned her Lexus into his driveway, anxiety welled up inside her.

After their argument at the beach, she and Ben had kissed and made up; then she'd gone home to shower and change. But she was still uncomfortable with what had transpired—she'd never expected Ben Birnbaum to be a possessive boyfriend, and she wasn't really sure how to handle it. And she felt equally uncomfortable, the closer she got to it, about a family dinner with parents. Ben had told her in great detail about the travails of his father, whose huge gambling addiction had sucked dry his enormous income from being plastic surgeon to the stars. It had led to an ugly incident on New Year's Eve and to Ben's mom being hospitalized with a nervous breakdown.

Now here it was, just a few weeks later. Mom was home, Dad was supposedly functional, and Ben had invited her to share a Friday night meal with them. Though she'd told Ben yes, by the time she was ringing the front door to his house, she was thinking a big fat *no.*

A maid opened the door and cheerfully invited Anna inside. Anna hadn't been sure what to wear for a meet-the-parents, so she'd gone with wardrobe staples: a gray cashmere sweater and black wool Chanel trousers.

The front hallway was adorned with photographs of Ben and his parents at various ages, as well as a few framed articles about Dr. Birnbaum from the *Los Angeles Times, New York Times,* and *Los Angeles* magazine. Anna was looking at this last one and reading how Dr. Birnbaum was the consensus best plastic surgeon in Los Angeles when Ben came bounding down the stairs, looking fabulous in a black T-shirt under an Armani jacket.

He hugged her and held her close. "How about if we just pretend this afternoon never happened?" he whispered into her hair.

Her answer was to nod and kiss him. But she noted that it wasn't the first time in recent memory that she'd been forced to erase the mental records on his behalf. She felt herself relax; everything was going to be all right.

"So listen," he went on, "my parents decided we should eat out. My dad made reservations at Spago; we're supposed to meet them there. That okay with you? It's not my favorite, but my dad thinks it's good for his business to be seen there."

"Are you sure you really want to have dinner with them?" Anna asked. "It's not too soon?"

"Nah. It was my idea. I really want them to meet you."

Anna swallowed uncomfortably. This was Ben's idea?

"Well . . . Spago sounds okay, I guess," she said. If she had to meet Ben's parents, neutral ground seemed less intimate.

Ben checked his watch. "We've got a little time. At the risk of sounding like I'm ten, want to see my room? It's been pretty much hermetically sealed since high school. Last year's BHH yearbook alone is worth the price of admission."

She nodded, so Ben led her upstairs, along a wide hallway, and then into his blue-carpeted bedroom. A large-screen plasma TV dominated one wall; a Sansui sound system, as well as floor-to-ceiling compartments full of CDs, lined another one. In the far corner was a well-equipped office and study area, complete with PC, color printer, and fax and answering machines.

Ben reached for some photo albums on a bookshelf; they sat on his bed to leaf through them. "Just remember, if I'm willing to let you see me looking like a weenie, you have to return the favor and show me your own geek-stage pictures."

She hesitated before nodding, because as far as she knew, she hadn't had a "geek" stage. Nonetheless, it warmed her heart to see snapshots of Ben playing Little League and as a Cub Scout in the troop at Temple

Emanuel in Beverly Hills. He even broke out his bar mitzvah pictures—it had been a lavish affair, to say the least. Anna recognized a younger and chubbier Sam sitting at a teen table with Dee. Cammie stood behind them, one hand on each of their shoulders, secure in her pubescent sensuality.

"Just one more set, then I'll put you out of your misery," he promised. "High school junior year, when I made the mistake of trying out for the school play. Here, look through these—I have to pee." He handed her one more photo album and kissed her forehead before departing for the bathroom.

She grinned as she turned the pages—there was Ben as Danny Zuko in *Grease,* decked out in a 1950s costume, his mouth opened wide to sing. That he wanted to share that part of himself with her was endearing, really.

Across the room Ben's phone rang three times. She didn't answer it—wouldn't have dreamed of answering it—then his machine picked up. Ben had left the volume turned up on the machine, so Anna couldn't help but overhear the message.

"Dude, it's your roomie Josh at Princeton. Dean Ward called me today to see if I'd heard anything from you about spring semester. She said she FedExed a letter to your house. Didja get it? Basically said if your ass isn't back here on Monday morning, you're out. So get it in gear, because I don't want them to give me some transfer student from Hofstra. Later."

The machine clicked off, leaving Anna stunned.

"Oops. Princeton is a thorough place," Ben said.

Anna turned. He was standing in the doorway, grinning sheepishly.

"What are you doing, Ben?" Anna demanded.

He shook his head. "How did we get here, Anna? How did this happen?"

"I don't know what you're talking about."

"Once I told you that I didn't know what love was, you remember?" He stepped into the room, then sat on his bed.

"Yes."

"Well, now I do. Isn't that a bitch?"

She still didn't understand. He tugged her gently to the bed. They sat side by side, and he stared into her eyes. "I didn't mean to fall in love with you, Anna, but it happened anyway. It's the most overwhelming, consuming thing, wonderful and terrible at the same time."

She opened her mouth to speak, but he raised his index finger to her lips. "And now that I know what love is," he continued, "I can't just walk away from it. Away from *you.*"

It was Anna's worst subconscious fear, articulated. "You haven't gone back to school because of *me?*"

He put a hand in her hair and held it away from her face. "You feel it, too. I know you do."

She did feel . . . something. But Ben's revelation didn't feel liberating—it felt quite the opposite. Yes, the earth had certainly moved more than once during the last few days. But she didn't want Ben to jettison his life because of it. What had happened to the self-confident boy to whom she had given her heart? Where was his center? Who was he? Clearly he didn't know. And it was easier to hang his life on her than to face his own self-doubts and insecurities.

"I only want what's best for you, Ben, I swear it. You have to go back to Princeton. You'll never forgive yourself if you don't. In the long run, you'll never forgive me, either."

"How do you know what I'll do?" he retorted. "Don't you hear what I'm telling you?"

"Ben, I think you're the one not hearing me. Don't you understand? You're smothering me."

He called his father to say they couldn't make it; then they sat in his boyhood room, talking for hours. Anna tried to convince him that the boy who'd lived in that room was gone and that the man he would become needed to move forward and have the courage to let her go.

By the end of the night there wasn't an emotion left unfelt. Anger, joy, sadness, fear. And of course, love. Lots of love. The evening ended with them making love by the moonlight streaming in through the open shutters.

And both of them knew it was for the very last time.

Crash Helmet

Ben looked around—the line of people waiting to go through the metal detectors and security screeners to reach the departure gates for American Airlines flights snaked back for several hundred feet. To his left was a prominent and threatening sign: ONLY TICKETED PASSENGERS BEYOND SECURITY. HAVE YOUR TICKET AND ID READY FOR INSPECTION.

"Not exactly like the movies," he said to Anna.

"What do you mean?"

"You know, Humphrey Bogart and Ingrid Bergman on the tarmac in *Casablanca*, plane revving in the background, music swelling, et cetera."

Anna managed a half smile. Even she had watched *Casablanca*, where heroic Humphrey Bogart loved Ingrid Bergman but made sure she got on the airplane because it was the best thing for her.

"Will you come visit?" Ben asked. "We could go skiing or snowboarding or rent a cabin in Vermont."

"Ben," she gently chided, then peered at him closely. "You gonna be okay?"

154

He grinned; it was the assurance that Anna needed. Then he gently nudged Anna's chin with his fist. "Here's looking at you, kid." He slung his backpack over his shoulder, turned, and walked away to join the security queue farthest from Anna. She stood for a moment, waiting to see if he would look back. He didn't. So she drifted away, edging through the crowds of travelers to go back to the parking structure and her car.

Getting out of LAX was easy. Getting home, though, was a pain in the ass. She'd been stuck in bumper-to-bumper traffic for a half hour when her cell phone rang. Normally she didn't answer when she was driving—Los Angeles drivers were dangerous enough without her being distracted on the phone. But bumper-to-bumper traffic that rolled along at three miles an hour maximum didn't seem particularly hazardous.

She answered. "Hello?"

"Hey, Sunshine, what's up?"

Anna recognized Danny's warm, upbeat voice.

"I'm at a dead stop on the 405, staring at the rear end of a Hummer that hasn't moved in five minutes. How about you?"

"Joy. On my way to Hugo's for lunch. Wanna join me?"

"Where's Hugo's?"

"Oh yeah, that's right. You're a newbie. Santa Monica Boulevard, West Hollywood. Serious industry hangout with awesome French toast and eight-buck oatmeal. Whaddaya say?"

"I say yes," Anna agreed impulsively. Why not? She really didn't want to go home to her father's empty house and brood. Besides, Danny was so upbeat, he could bring anyone out of a funk. "It might take a while, though; traffic's barely moving."

"Take the 405 to Santa Monica Boulevard, then go east. It's on the left-hand side—you can't miss it."

"How long?"

"Thirty minutes. Just look for the Jewish guy with the big nose, with three, four babes hanging on my every word. Or my laptop. Take your pick."

She said goodbye, hung up, and smiled. Danny was definitely the antidote she needed. As it turned out, Hugo's French toast turned out to be a close second—sizzling golden brown, with fresh California strawberries and homemade whipped cream. During their lunch at least five people stopped by their table to say hello—mostly other writers who knew Danny. But Danny also took her over to meet someone named Dick Wolf, the producer of the *Law & Order* cop dramas. Anna had never heard of him, but Danny assured her that he was one of the most powerful men in Hollywood.

To everyone Danny said that Anna was "from Apex." Anna was surprised at how much respect this introduction reaped. No one looked fazed by Anna's young age.

"This is a young town," Danny confided as he took out a credit card to pay their check. "Live fast, die young, write your scripts in eight days max."

"I think I'd prefer to live medium and take a year to write a novel," Anna confessed.

"Then maybe you haven't really lived," Danny said as the waitress took his credit card. "What's the fastest you've ever driven a car?"

"What kind of question is that?"

"Just curious. How fast?

Anna thought for a moment. When she was seventeen, she'd been in Germany with her mother. One time, on one of the autobahns, she'd cajoled her mother into letting her drive and had gotten the speed up to a hundred forty kilometers—about eighty-four miles an hour.

"Eighty-five. About."

Danny threw his head back and laughed.

"What's so funny?"

"Nothing," Danny told her. "Come on, I've got something to show you."

Ninety minutes later the two of them were standing in a sizable garage in Riverside, California, about sixty miles from Los Angeles. More specifically, at the Riverside race course. Danny had explained to Anna on the drive there that Riverside had hosted some of the most important automobile races in the world. Though its heyday had been a few decades before, the track was still open to people who had the nerve—and the money—to pay to use it.

"And this," Danny said, "is my baby until such time as I have an actual one. At which point I'm confident that my wife will insist that I sell it." With a huge flourish he grabbed one end of a tarpaulin sheet that covered one of the sports cars in the garage and yanked. The tarp flew off, revealing an open-cockpit, white classic sports car with a roll bar behind the driver's side. There was a number 8 painted on the door and the words *Little Bastard* in script just above the number.

Anna, who knew nothing about cars or racing, knew she had to make some suitable comment. "Nice."

"Nice?" Danny mock-challenged her. "Nice? Lunch at Hugo's is nice. Hermosa Beach—the town, not the show—is nice. But this? This is an exact replica of the same Porsche Spyder that James Dean owned. And died in on September 30, 1955, right near Paso Robles, on his way to a race in Salinas. But that accident wasn't his fault."

Danny took a key out of his pocket and tossed it to her. "It's all yours."

"You mean, you want me to drive it?"

"Can you handle a stick?"

"Sure."

"You're older than eighteen?"

Anna nodded.

"Then why not?" Danny went to a shelf and took down a couple of crash helmets. "As long as you're willing to sign a release for the track and wear one of these."

Five minutes later Anna, having signed the release, was in the driver's seat with Danny riding shotgun as they tooled out of the garage and onto the track. The starter gave Anna an all-clear signal, meaning that there was no other raceway traffic for her to worry about.

"Go for it," Danny told her.

Anna put her foot down, and the engine roared. The first time around she drove cautiously, getting the Spyder up to eighty miles an hour or so on the backstretch but staying well under that through the turns. The second time, though, the sports car seemed to be urging her to go faster and faster. Anna answered its call on the front stretch. Eighty. Ninety. A hundred. A hundred and ten, a hundred and twenty miles an hour!

"That's it!" Danny encouraged her. "No highway patrol here!"

There was a left-hand curve coming out of the straightaway, and Anna downshifted to handle the turn with ease.

"Nice job there," said Danny. "I didn't know you had it in you."

Anna smiled, keeping her eyes on the track. "Neither did I. Let's do it again."

"Letting an Upper East Side trust fund princess drive my Spyder. My grandfather, may he rest in peace, would turn over in his grave at Mount Sinai Cemetery."

Anna loved the way Danny made her laugh. The more she got to know him, the more she liked him. She knew it wasn't the Cyn-would-be-so-proud-of-me kind of extraordinary passion she'd felt with Ben. That had been amazing, and she'd always treasure her memories of Ben.

This was something else. And it felt really, really good.

Long Red Talons

Three hours later, Anna was on the set of *Hermosa Beach* while Danny was laboring away in the writers' room. While they were in Riverside, the call from Clark had come, ordering them both to come to work. Never mind that Saturday had been declared a day off for the staff, who had worked for fifteen straight days, and that no one was supposed to come in until that evening. Clark had decided the show was behind schedule, so the scenes that were to have been taped on Sunday were being shot today. No questions asked.

Today's filming was on a small stretch of Hermosa Beach that had been closed to the general public. Nonetheless, a thick ring of tourists had gathered around the roped-off, heavily guarded perimeter, snapping photos to take back home to Boise or Duluth or Edinburgh, where their tale of having watched a television show being filmed was a very big deal. (The only people who hated the filming were the Hermosa Beach locals, who were certain that their multi-million-dollar beach homes came with an inalienable right to the entire beachfront all the time. This despite the fact that half of them earned sizable livings in that very same entertainment industry.)

Anna stood near the director—a short man in a Dodgers baseball cap and sunglasses who seemed pathologically opposed to smiling. She held a script plus a sheaf of papers that listed everyone's attire down to the last detail. With some of the production aides sidelined with a stomach bug, Anna's job today was to check and recheck every character's hair, wardrobe, and accessories for continuity. Basically it was her responsibility to make sure that if a character had her hair parted on the right, it stayed on the right.

The scene they were currently shooting came after a party in the hotel ballroom. In that sequence Chyme had run crying from the party after seeing Cruise kissing Alexandra. Now Alexandra would confront Chyme; they'd argue for a while, then Chyme would storm off down the beach. And then Cruise would come outside to look for her, only to be seduced by the ever-scheming Alexandra.

Anna ran down her detailed list. Chyme's hair was entwined with a rope of pearls—check. The pearls were the same delicate oyster shade as her elegant Atelier Versace lace gown—check. Tiffany white gold "Anastasia Diva" chandelier earrings set with diamonds—check. Shoes, cosmetics—everything matched the previous shot.

She moved on to Alexandra, who wore a red Gucci

corset dress. (Bad choice, Anna thought. The dress was another one far too obvious for a girl of Alexandra's background.) Gunmetal leather-and-crystal T-strap Spaulding & Gublo sandals—check. Tiffany diamond hoop earrings that Anna also thought were wrong since Alexandra would never wear such large earrings— check. Short nails with no polish—

Shit.

Somehow Alexandra's nails had morphed once again into long red talons that could do bodily harm to lower life-forms. Anna checked and rechecked her detail sheet. Short nails, clear nail polish. It was plain as day.

"Set up for the kiss, please!" called the director.

The kiss. Meaning the moment where Cruise ran out to the beach and Alexandra kissed him. Which most likely meant a close-up of those killer crimson talons curled into Cruise's thick, dark hair.

Anna looked around for the designer in charge of hair and makeup, but he was nowhere to be found. Neither was Danny. So she took a deep breath and hurried over to the director himself, who was huddled in a conference with two of his assistants.

"Sir?" Anna asked.

"What?" the director barked. "And who are you?"

"An intern," Anna explained. "Sorry to interrupt, but . . ." She showed him that her detail sheet called for Alexandra to have short, clear nails. "I don't think that's what she has."

The director stared at Alexandra. "You're right.

Of all the childish— She knows better than that," he said with disgust. "'Scuse me. We're on hold, people! Take ten!"

The director tracked down the makeup artist, who'd miraculously reappeared with her bag of cosmetic tricks. She trotted over to Pegasus to give her a nail redo. Pegasus shot a lethal look in Anna's direction.

"Hey, nice catch on the nail thing," the first AD called to Anna.

Anna smiled. It was good to feel useful for a change.

"So can I be in it?" Mia asked Clark.

Mia had managed to wedge herself between Cammie and Clark when they'd all gotten into his limo to go to the set of *Hermosa Beach.*

"No, you can't be in it," Clark chided her gently.

"Why not?" Mia shot back. "I can act."

Clark chuckled. "Were you in school plays or something?"

"No, but I know I can act," Mia insisted. "So can I be in it?"

Cammie stared out the window and watched Los Angeles pass by. The only reason she'd come on this outing was to ensure that her father and Mia wouldn't bond in her absence. But she still tried to put Mia out of her mind, preferring to think about, say, Adam.

He couldn't get over his amazing luck the night before at being treated to a private concert by Beck and Willie Nelson—Cammie had joined him for the last half hour of it—and he was exceedingly grateful to Cammie for having brought him to the after party. Naturally he'd happily accepted her invitation to her birthday bash on Tuesday night. He had not, however, suggested that he drive her home and hadn't offered more than a warm hug when they parted. Well, Cammie was sure that in Adam's mind, a hug was the gentlemanly thing to do. He was the kind of guy who probably didn't French-kiss until a third date. At that rate she calculated that Adam's intro to down and dirty wouldn't happen until graduation. However *American Pie* that might be, Cammie planned to accelerate the learning curves.

The limo stopped by the beach; Clark hopped out without waiting for his driver to open the door. Mia and Cammie scrambled after him as he strode across the sand toward the roped-off area where *Hermosa Beach* was filming. The gawkers began taking photos of Cammie, certain she was Somebody. She ignored them, scanning the area for the enemy.

She found her—Anna—with a short guy who wore jeans and a T-shirt and carried a small steno-style note-book. Obviously a writer. So Cammie slapped a big smile on her face and marched over to join them. "Hi, Anna," she said, oozing sweetness. "I guess Dad has you working on a Saturday, huh?"

"That's all right," Anna said coolly. "Do you know Danny Bluestone?"

"You mean the guy with the notebook?" Cammie asked.

Anna introduced them. Like Cammie cared. But she gave The Notebook a sexy smile just the same. What the hell, maybe he'd turn out to be important one day. In the meantime Mia bopped over to join them, her arm looped through Clark's.

"Hey, did anyone ever tell you that you look just like Gwyneth Paltrow?" Mia asked Anna, wide-eyed. "Swear to God."

"I'll take that as a compliment," Anna said graciously.

"So what part do you play?" Mia asked.

"I'm not an actress; I'm Mr. Sheppard's intern."

"I'm his daughter!" Mia exclaimed.

Daughter? Cammie's eyebrows headed for the sky. *Stepdaughter.* But Clark didn't correct Mia. Instead he grinned.

"We're a big happy family, that's for sure. So, everything all set for Jackson?"

The Notebook nodded. "We should be able to shoot his scene right after sunset. Then *Hollywood Tonight* is coming to cover the beach party."

Clark looked nervously at a bank of clouds on the western horizon. "If the damn weather doesn't fuck us. I promised Jackson we could do him in under an hour. Then an hour of partying for the press and he's back to his pregnant wife."

Cammie could think of only one "Jackson" who would merit that much concern from her father. "Are you talking about Jackson Sharpe?"

"I'm sure as hell not talking about Michael Jackson."

Her father snorted, looking through some papers The Notebook handed him.

"Jackson Sharpe is shooting a scene tonight for *Hermosa Beach*?" Cammie clarified.

Her father looked up from the papers. "Yeah, so?"

So? Cammie's supposed best friend's dad was doing a cameo on Cammie's father's show and Sam hadn't even *mentioned* it?

"How's our schedule?" Clark barked at The Notebook.

"We're one scene behind," Danny reported. "But Anna saved our ass today." He explained the continuity problem with Alexandra's nails.

"Good job, Anna." Clark grunted, shielding his eyes from the sun with his hand.

Danny nudged a playful elbow into Anna's side. "From Clark Sheppard, that's tantamount to a coronation."

Cammie knew she should be seething but actually just felt morose and lonely. Here was Anna, getting compliments from her dad, flirting with The Notebook, and Ben Birnbaum was probably at home at the top of Stone Canyon, waiting for her. After that, Anna would probably call Sam and meet her—and probably Dee, too—for dinner at the Hotel Bel Air and then drive down to Encounter at the airport for after-dinner drinks.

Who could cheer her up? Her thoughts returned to Adam. Even though that first kiss she gave him was just to make Sam jealous, now she thought about him a lot. His tenderness. His humor. He was just so . . . so decent. And under that good-boy facade, she knew there had to be a very bad boy in all the ways that counted; she could tell by the way he'd kissed her back. Funny, though. When she pictured them together, they weren't doing the nasty. Instead her head rested on his shoulder while he stroked her hair.

For once Cammie didn't want to prove to a guy how hot she was. Instead she just wanted the guy.

Comedy

S am piled her plate with broiled lobster tails, prawns wrapped in bacon, smoked salmon, and the kind of *pomme frites* that were only made in Paris bistros or by a chef hired away from one. After a few days of Power Eating, Sam had chucked in the towel. Yes, she wanted to be skinny, but not at the price of food that tasted like it had already been digested. She couldn't quite decide if her own unwillingness to suffer for beauty meant that she was a hopeless sloth or that she was showing a new maturity. Maybe she'd have to ask her psychiatrist, Dr. Fred. Of course, she'd once looked up from the couch to see him nibbling on an Atkins bar.

As she took a bite of delicious aged Brie cheese, she mused how the *Hermosa Beach* festivities hadn't turned out to be much of a beach party. The skies had opened up right after her father had completed his scene, where he played himself as an arriving guest at the hotel. This was called "stunt casting," and Jackson had done it as a favor to Clark Sheppard. What Jackson was paying Clark back for Sam could only imagine.

In any case, the beach party had been moved into the hotel lobby. Sam watched her father hold court in his easy way on an aqua velvet couch as the camera crew from *Hollywood Tonight* set up to interview him. When he wasn't with her pregnant bimbo of a stepmother, Sam quite liked her father, despite the fact that they rarely spent time together. But Sam had high hopes that the new movie she was going to make with Anna would change all that. She reminded herself to talk to Anna again about writing a script for it.

Hoisting her very full plate, still chewing on the Brie, Sam walked past the bar, where muscled bartenders dressed as lifeguards served up red apple martinis in glasses rimmed with crushed peppermint candy. And then past the dessert tables, piled with miniature versions of every Viennese torte known to mankind. Across the lobby she saw Anna with a young guy with glasses and Clark with a young teen. She cast her eyes around for Cammie, surprised she wasn't there. Now that she thought about it, though, she and Cammie hadn't talked about this party. In fact, she realized, recently she and Cammie hadn't done a lot of talking at—

"Mind if I join you?"

Sam looked up into the marine eyes of a guy so handsome he took her breath away. Or maybe she was just choking on the cheese. She gasped for breath, coughing hoarsely.

The guy hit her on the back. "You okay? Need a Heimlich maneuver?"

Sam managed to shake her head. The guy found an apple martini and gave it to Sam, who sipped gratefully. "Sorry. Went down the wrong pipe."

"Hey, it happens." He sat down and held out his hand, indicating that Sam should sit in the empty seat next to it. "I'm Shayne Weston."

"Sam," she said, leaving off the Sharpe. Usually she played up her famous name. But for some reason, at this moment, she didn't. Now that he was sitting down, she could get a read on this guy: Brad Pitt circa *Thelma and Louise* crossed with Chris Klein circa *Election*. "You must be an actor."

"That obvious, huh?" He grinned disarmingly.

"Are you on the show?" Sam asked.

"Three episodes. I'm a lifeguard who saves Chyme's life. She cries on my shoulder over Cruise's engagement to Alexandra and we fall into each other's arms until she finds out that I'm only getting close to her so that I can discover the combination to her father's safe."

"Oh, you're the lifeguard who's really a burglar," Sam said, laughing. "Now, that's innovative writing."

"I hear it came from Clark Sheppard, not the writers' room. Anyway, my agent says it might become a continuing role. You never know."

He popped a chunk of melon in his mouth. Sam felt suddenly self-conscious about the mountain of fattening food on her plate. She set it on the table behind her.

"So, my turn," Shayne said. "You're an actress, right?"

"God, no," Sam said, though she was flattered. "Actually I'm a director."

His eyebrows went up. "Yeah? Have I seen your work?"

Sam shrugged nonchalantly. "I'm working on a new film now."

"Wow." He looked impressed. "I would've thought you were still in college, maybe grad school or something."

Sam took another sip of her martini, feeling as sophisticated as the drink. This was cool. She really must be looking more mature these days. "Not college," she told him. Which was true enough.

"So how'd you end up at this party?" Shayne asked.

Sam shrugged again. "Friends."

He nodded and leaned toward her, studying her face. "Man, you have the greatest eyes."

"I do?" Sam was taken aback. No guy had ever complimented her eyes before. They were brown. Big deal. She'd tried colored contact lenses but had only succeeded in looking like a brown-eyed girl pathetic enough to wear fake blue eyes.

"Oh yeah. Guys must tell you that all the time."

Sam tried a noncommittal smile. His face was so close to hers. He smelled of some subtle, spicy cologne. Okay, this boy was seriously hot. It almost made her chuckle to think that not very long ago, she'd worried that she might be gay. No girl could make her feel this kind of heat.

"Hey, I'd really like to get to know you better," Shayne went on. "Maybe we could have lunch, catch a movie. Or am I moving too fast here—?"

"Uh-uh." She took her MAC Spice lip pencil out of her purse, wrote her cell number on her napkin, and handed it to him.

"Great." Shayne tucked it in the pocket of his jeans and got up from his seat. Sam watched as one of his drunk friends came lurching toward him.

"Hey, Shayno Bane-o! How's it goin', bro?"

"Hey, Greg," Shayne said back. "You been hittin' the juice a little too hard, bud?"

The drunk guy loomed over Shayne. "They're fuckin' great," he slurred. "You should definitely try one." He took a long sip from his martini glass. "So Shayno Bane-o, you find Jackson Sharpe's daughter like I tol' you?"

Shit. Shit, shit, shit. Sam could see from Shayne's face that his wasted bud had just busted him. He'd known all along who she was. That was why he'd tried to pick her up. Because he was under the false impression that dating Jackson Sharpe's daughter would help his talentless ass. It had happened to her so often; how could she be so stupid as to fall for it *again*? Well, screw both of them. Sam stood up, glaring at the two guys. Then she used her impressive lungs to make sure her voice would carry across the hotel's lobby.

"I don't care about your gay porn videos, *Shayne*. I don't call that a reel of your work. Sorry!" She could see heads swivel in their direction; exactly the reason she had done it.

"You bitch," he hissed at her.

"Fuck you very much," she spat, and walked away.

Danny Bluestone was in the middle of telling Anna a truly hilarious story about Clark and the producers locking the writing staff in the room one night until they came up with new beats for a story line when Anna saw Sam bolt down the hall toward the production offices.

"Danny, could you excuse me a minute?" Anna stood and followed Sam, who ducked into one of the two restrooms at the end of the corridor. Anna entered to find Sam in one of the stalls, her chin in her hands.

"We can't go on meeting like this," Sam joked, since the first time she and Anna had spoken had been in the ladies' room at her father's wedding. Sam had been in tears then, too.

"Anything interesting playing in here?" Anna said with a smile.

"Actually, my entire fucked-up existence. I just can't decide if it's a tragedy or a comedy."

"What happened?"

"Am I a stupid girl?" Sam demanded.

"You know the answer to that."

"Right. I'm smart. Very. So would you please tell me why I fall for some putz with a line and believe he likes me when all he wants is access to my dad?"

Ah. So that was it. Anna knew it happened to Sam all the time. But to be fair, Sam traded on her father's name all the time, too. "Come on. Let's go for a walk," Anna suggested.

"It's raining."

"We'll take umbrellas. There's a back way out; we don't have to go through the party."

Anna got the umbrellas from a utility closet and led Sam to a rear door, which opened into an alley. They followed it to the asphalt walk that paralleled the beach. Though everything was still wet, the rain had stopped, so the umbrellas weren't necessary.

Save for the two of them, the walk was empty. They strolled for eight or ten minutes in silence before Anna spoke. "So, some butt head in there tried to take you for a ride. . . ."

Sam nodded. "A very hot one who temporarily made me forget the real world where my thighs suffocate each other every time I take a step."

Anna bit back a laugh, sure Sam was in no mood to have her sense of humor appreciated. "You can't go by Beverly Hills standards. Everyone is crazy here."

"Please." Sam snorted. "Only thin chicks ever say that."

"Sam, you're not fat!"

"But I'm not thin. And not beautiful. And I never will be."

"Sam, you're judging by crazy Hollywood standards. You're in the wrong city. In New York, I know a dozen guys who'd be all over you. Because you're the whole package."

"Great. I'm a three-thousand-mile mistake."

Anna *had* to laugh at that one. "There's got to be something that's more important to you than obsessing about your looks." They turned off the walk and onto the Strand, passing Dublin's and the other rollicking nightspots. Music wafted out of open doors.

Sam nodded. "Yeah, there's more important stuff. Making movies, maybe."

"Like the one we're allegedly working on together?" Anna teased.

Sam had the grace to look chagrined. "I might have overstated the situation in class. But did you see how excited everyone was?"

"Yes. But that's not why I want to do it with you."

Sam's face lit up. "You do?"

"I don't love being Clark Sheppard's intern. But I did love writing those monologues. So if you think I have any talent—"

"Hell, yes!" Sam exclaimed. "Any ideas for a plot?"

"Now that I know we're really going to try, I'll think about it, okay?"

"Absolutely, partner." Sam stopped walking and turned to Anna. She held out her hand, and Anna shook it, with a solemnity that made Sam smile. "You take this stuff seriously."

"Yeah. Don't you?"

"Yeah," Sam agreed. They started walking again. "I

want to do something important. Does that sound pretentious?"

Anna shook her head. "Not to me."

"Me neither," Sam mused. "I've lived here my entire life and I haven't met anyone who'd agree with me about that." She stopped again to peer at Anna. "Except you."

Mo Bad

Adam felt slightly ridiculous sitting next to Cammie in the passenger seat while she zoomed at eighty miles an hour south on the 405 toward Hermosa Beach. But both of his parents were out, which meant there was no family car to borrow.

Just get over it, he told himself. Feeling like you have to be in the driver's seat is some macho thing left over from another century. When he and Anna had been together, she'd almost always been the one to drive, and—

Anna. It was like she was constantly hovering on the edge of his consciousness. His eyes slid over to Cammie, who was softly singing along to the Beck CD on her awesome sound system.

Why she'd suddenly gotten interested in him—if, in fact, she really was interested—was a question to which he had no answer. She'd called him an hour earlier and invited him to a party on the set of *Hermosa Beach*, the new TV show that her father had packaged. She'd caught him in his room, staring at a blank computer screen. He was supposed to be writing a paper on *The Scarlet Letter*. Adam had found it a monumentally depressing novel: Hester Prynne had done the deed with Dimmesdale and gotten marked for life. It was the moral equivalent of an incurable STD. Maybe that was why he'd jumped at the chance to hang out with Cammie, who apparently was missing the guilt gene altogether.

"So, am I Mr. January?" popped out of his mouth.

Cammie's eyes flicked to him, then back to the road. She turned down Beck's wail. "Pardon me?"

Adam shrugged. "I figure you have a different guy every month."

A smile played on her lips. "Maybe I just like you. Can't it ever be that simple?"

"With you?" Adam asked. "My guess is: rarely."

She laughed and gunned the car to ninety. Which caused Adam to give himself another mental: what the hell. If January was his month, he might as well sit back and enjoy it.

As for Cammie, her mind worked overtime as she motored her car down the narrow streets that led to Hermosa Beach. Adam presumed he was her flavor of the month. Well, maybe he was. All she knew was that being at the set with her dad and Mia, and watching her father fawn over Anna Percy, was not her idea of a good time. So she'd called Adam and invited him to the party, then gotten her dad's driver to take her home so she could get her own car. And then she'd gone to get Adam—who didn't have a car of his own—and then driven all the way back to the hotel again. It was so *not* her style.

Whatever. She liked Adam. There was no reason to be coy about it.

By the time they arrived, the party that had been meandering an hour and a half before was in full swing. Mo Bad, an up-and-coming hip-hop star—and another Apex client—was doing his thing on a small stage that had been set up during the time Cammie had been gone. Mo wore twelve heavy gold chains around his neck instead of a shirt; his muscles rippled under ebony skin and his boxers showed a good two inches above his pants. Cammie knew for a fact that Mo wasn't from the streets; in fact, he'd grown up rich in Santa Monica and had attended Harvard-Westlake, arguably the snootiest private school in Los Angeles.

Dancing behind Mo were two women who wore nothing but thongs. They had been dipped, head to toe, in chocolate. Bor-ing. Cammie had already seen the choco-chicks at two holiday parties that season. They were so five minutes ago. Out on the dance floor a girl with choppy dark hair lifted her Bebe T-shirt to expose a pair of perfect breasts. Yawn. Like having perfect tits in Los Angeles was something special.

"There's Sam," Adam said, bobbing his head toward one side of the dance floor, where Sam was dancing with the writer Cammie had met earlier, the one she'd dubbed The Notebook. Cammie glanced around. No Anna, which made her mood improve appreciably. But she didn't feel like talking to Sam, or Mia, or her father. All she felt like doing was being in Adam's arms.

Mo gave her a chance when he took a break and another young singer took the mike. She crooned a husky ballad as she accompanied herself on guitar. Several couples began to slow dance. Cammie took Adam's hand and led him to the dance floor and then slinked her arms around his neck. His arms snaked around her waist. He moved really well—had to be the athlete in him.

"We fit," she purred, smiling up at him.

"I bet you said that to Mr. December," he replied.

"No, actually I didn't."

His smile was endearingly crooked. "Come on, Cammie. I know you. You go for those bad-boy types. And that isn't me."

"Maybe you just never had enough motivation," Cammie teased, her voice heavy with innuendo.

"Maybe I don't want to play those little games you thrive on," Adam replied.

She pressed closer to him, both annoyed that he refused to flirt with her and impressed that he could resist it. "You think you know me, but you don't, Adam. I barely know myself."

Suddenly Cammie felt Adam stiffen. Now Cammie saw why: Anna was slow dancing with The Notebook and looking really happy about it. She heard Adam curse softly under his breath. And suddenly she felt uncharacteristically protective of him.

"Did you know she was going to be here? Is that what this is about?" he asked.

"No, Adam. Not at all. Anna's interning for my dad, so she and I are bound to be invited to the same functions. But I didn't want to let her get in the way of my seeing you tonight. I hope that's okay with you."

"Of course it is. I didn't mean to wig out on you."

"Don't worry about it. And whatever you do, do *not* worry about Anna's new-*new-new* boyfriend," she counseled.

"What happened to Ben?" Adam asked, a muscle jumping in his jaw.

"Beats me."

Adam shook his head. "I don't get her. First she wants to be alone, then she wants to be with Ben, now she wants to be with this dude. . . ."

At that moment Cammie saw Anna staring at them over The Notebook's not-very-tall shoulder. So she narrowed her eyes in a way that said, "Guess who's with the better guy?" then rested her head against Adam's broad, muscular shoulder.

Danny reached a hand out to Anna and helped her into one of the horse-drawn carriages that were lined up on the street outside the hotel—a special touch for the party. Giddy from two martinis and Danny's sense of humor, Anna had readily agreed to a carriage ride. It would be fun. And it meant she wouldn't have to look at Cammie with Adam. The sight of them together had come close to ruining her evening. He was a great guy. She was a scorpion. Anna knew that it was only a matter of time before Adam got stung.

The carriage driver gave them a cashmere throw—Danny and Anna settled under it as the coachman urged his two horses forward. Horseshoes click-clocked against asphalt.

"Warm enough?" Danny wrapped an arm around Anna.

"Fine," she replied. The apple martinis had a powerful kick, and Anna wasn't much of a drinker. "Right now it's probably absolute zero in New York. But here in La La Land, you can eat oranges off the tree in January."

"I hate New York. I'm such a California guy, I'd turn into the Iceman in that kind of weather."

"Ah, yes. But would the Iceman cometh?" Anna teased, impressed with her sudden bawdiness.

Danny raised one eyebrow. "That, my dear, has yet to be determined. And did Anna Percy just let fly with a risqué pun?"

"It must be the air in California. Or the martinis," Anna allowed. "Or both. They'll never let me back in New York City again. Anyway, I never liked that play. All those drunks nourishing illusions and wasting their lives."

"You know a better writer than Eugene O'Neill?" Danny asked.

"You!" Anna said, a bit drunk herself. "Let's talk about your novel."

"The one I haven't started? Let's talk about yours."

The carriage turned south, heading toward the pier. "A woman goes to battle against a giant eunuch of a white whale," she began solemnly. "I call it: *Moby Dick-less.*"

Danny laughed really hard. Which got Anna laughing, too. She turned to him, wiping tears of mirth from her eyes. His hand lifted her chin. Then his lips were on hers in the sweetest of kisses.

I don't love him, Anna thought. But right at this moment, I'm happy. What's wrong with that?

So she pulled Danny close and kissed him back.

Mo-Theo

"Yo, I know you from somewhere?"

Cammie was just returning from the ladies' room when Mo Bad called to her from his perch on a thronelike yellow wicker chair.

"Yo, no," Cammie replied, and kept on walking. Adam was out there alone, which made Cammie nervous. She wouldn't put it past Anna to blow off The Notebook and go back after Adam.

"Seriously," Mo said, sidling up to Cammie. "I seen you somewheres, you know what I'm sayin'? You lookin' hot, girl."

"They teach you to fake that ghetto crap at Harvard-Westlake?" Cammie asked with a sweet smile.

Mo scowled. "Where you be thinkin' I'm from, girl?"

"Whatever." Cammie stood on the toes of her Jimmy Choo boots and scanned the area for Adam.

"You lookin' for that tall dude you was grindin' on befo'?" Mo asked.

"Actually, I'm looking for Jesus," Cammie replied. "I

just had a spiritual epiphany. Not that you have a clue what that is."

"Shee-it," he drawled. "Sudden awakening, like that. You be judging me by my speech and shit."

Cammie folded her arms and stared him down. "Do you have any idea who I am? My father's firm is your agent."

Mo grinned. "For real? That's cool. You got a name?"

"If you'll drop the I'm-Tupac-reincarnated routine, I'll tell you."

He shrugged. "Fine by me," he said in a perfectly normal voice.

"It's Cammie."

"Nice to make your acquaintance, Cammie. My name is Theo, but don't let it get around. And you really are one beautiful girl."

"Thank you, and no, I'm not interested."

"Too bad. I was going to invite you and your boyfriend to a rave."

Cammie almost laughed out loud. "Excuse me? A rave? What would you know about that? And hello—1999 was a few years ago."

"Not this kind of rave. Take my word for it." Mo-Theo was a good head taller than Cammie. "An' I see your guy."

"Where?" she demanded.

"Near the front door. Talking to some tall, skinny blond chick."

Tall, skinny blond chick? It had to be Anna.

"In a T-shirt?"

"Affirmative," Mo-Theo said. "Why don't you ditch him and come with me to this party?"

Cammie made an instant decision. She wasn't going to allow Adam to get reeled back into Anna's poisonous clutches. "The second half was right," she told Mo. "Lemme get my boyfriend. We'd love to come."

Mo put on his oversized leather Fubu jacket and they headed for Adam. But when they got there, Cammie was relieved to see that it wasn't Anna at all— just a tall, skinny blonde with bad skin who she'd never seen before in her life. Adam introduced her as Sherrie, one of the production assistants on *Hermosa Beach.* And Sherrie proceeded to launch into a long and involved story about her upcoming wedding in Houston to a guy she'd known since kindergarten.

Cammie felt a little better. Then she realized that Anna Percy herself could reappear at any moment. "Guess what?" she asked Adam when Sherrie took a breath. "We're going to another party."

Adam checked his watch. "It's kind of late, isn't it?"

Mo-Theo laughed. "Is this boy for real?"

It wasn't unusual for girls at Beverly Hills High to hook up with hot guys from the proverbial wrong side of the tracks, which was why Cammie could attest to have attended a goodly number of parties in east L.A. Personally, Cammie found the rich-white-girl-hooks-up-with-the-Latino-son-of-Mexican-immigrants thing kind of played. But she dutifully followed Mo's 1995 Dodge Viper to the Echo Park neighborhood, where they parked outside an abandoned redbrick building in a dirt parking lot already jammed with SUVs and European sedans.

"Are you sure this is cool?" Adam asked, checking out the low-rent environs.

Cammie made her voice as manly as possible. "Don't worry, Adam. I'll protect you."

He laughed and draped an arm around her shoulders as they followed Mo across the street to the brick building. Mo rapped on the heavy metal door. It was opened by a scowling bald guy who had to be at least six-foot six, three hundred pounds. When he saw who was there, the scowl changed to a welcoming nod. "Yo, Mo, wazzup?"

They shared some kind of fist bump, then the big guy waved them all inside. Down a flight of stairs they entered a huge basement room. It teemed with young bodies dancing to pounding hip-hop. Red strobe lights blinked on and off. In a glass booth a DJ rocked out to the tunes he was sampling. The air was heavy with smoke from Columbia's finest and cigarettes.

Before she could say no, Mo dragged Cammie into the middle of the dancers. Not that she could have heard herself say no. Adam followed, and Cammie flirted with both of them as she danced, mesmerized by the sweaty groove. It was fun in a mindless, exhibitionist sort of way.

Mo leaned close. "Yo, you wanna do some E?"

E as in Ecstasy, as in MDMA. Ugh. Cammie was no stranger to felonious substances but had seen too many girls do E and decide instantly that they were madly in love with whatever boy happened to be in their immediate vicinity. She was much too much of a control freak to find that attractive.

She shook her head no; Mo responding by taking her hips and gyrating them against his. Cammie decided that she'd had enough of her father's client: she turned to Adam and threw her arms around his neck, slithering up and down as she danced. He stayed loose and sexy, didn't try too hard. And he seemed to be getting into it as much as Cammie was. The beat segued faster. More bodies pressed onto the dance floor. Nearby a girl took off her top and flung it into the crowd, then French-kissed the girl she was with.

Cammie turned around and danced with her back to Adam. The next thing she knew, she felt his arms around her waist from behind. He was still dancing but holding her fast. She looked over her shoulder; he seemed mesmerized by the dark, smoky, sexy room. She lifted her face to his and kissed him. He tasted salty as he turned her all the way toward him. She felt his hand under her butt, lifting her higher as he kissed her back; she wrapped her legs around him and just let herself go with the feeling. God, she'd been right. Adam Flood was hot! Really, really hot! He knew just how to kiss her and touch her and tease her. All she wanted to do was to rip his clothes off and—

"Cammie? Oh my God, *Cammie!*"

Suddenly Adam put her down. The spell was broken. Standing with them now, her eyes shining, was none other than Dee. She looked even more waifish than usual in a semi-transparent baby doll dress that showed off a pink bra and thong. "Wow, this is so cool!" Dee cried. "What a coincidence! How'd you get here?"

"The *Hermosa Beach* party!" Cammie yelled over the music.

"You were there? Me too!" Dee exclaimed. "Isn't it like the most awesome thing ever? I mean, I feel so in tune with everyone here. It's just so soulful!"

Cammie nodded. It was hard to tell whether Dee was on one of her New Age rants or had found her way to the E that Mo-Theo had mentioned.

"Wow, Adam, hi!" Dee gave him a huge hug. She looked from Cammie to Adam and back at Cammie. "Are you two . . . you know!"

"She's having my baby," Adam said with mock sincerity.

Dee took him seriously and clasped Cammie's arm. "Wow! Wait until I tell your sister!"

"What sister?" Cammie spat.

"Mia, silly," Dee said. "She's here, too. We met at the party, and these really cute guys invited us to come with them, and here we are!"

"You brought Mia to this place?" Cammie yelped.

"Come on, we went to parties like this when we

were fourteen," Dee reminded her. "You *gave* parties like this when you were fourteen."

"Where is she, Dee?" Cammie demanded. She knew that her stepsister was used to parties in the valley, where frat bizkits, aka frat boy wanna-bes still in high school, got drunk and threw up in someone's swimming pool. Mia was not ready to handle *this*.

Dee put her little fists on her hips. "How could I possibly know, Cammie?"

Cammie spoke directly into Adam's ear, shouting to be heard over the music. "We have to find my stepsister!"

"Who?"

"I'll explain later." She swung back around to Dee "Where's the last place you saw her?"

"Back there. Don't worry, she's totally safe!"

Cammie and Adam pushed through the gyrating bodies to look for Mia—Cammie told Adam to start by looking for red hair. But there was no sign of the young girl. They found themselves in a narrow hallway with a long line to use one of two functioning toilets. Cammie pounded on the bathroom doors—each opened to an irate partygoer, but neither was Mia.

"What now?" Adam asked.

"Outside!" Cammie declared. They found a fire exit at the end of the corridor and pushed it open.

There, on the ground, was Mia.

Glassy-eyed and out of it, Mia had mascara tracks running down both her cheeks. One of Cammie's favorite sweaters was half on and half off her shoulders.

Cammie grabbed her arm. "What did you take?"

Mia's head lolled. "Huh?"

"Who the hell are you?" A scruffy guy in his early twenties suddenly appeared, a half-consumed pint of Jack Daniels in his left hand.

"Her sister, you shit," Cammie told him. "She's fourteen."

The guy faltered. "Whoa. She told me she was *eighteen*."

"Get her out of here," Cammie ordered Adam, who lifted Mia and carried her around the building to Cammie's car.

"What are you doing?" Mia asked dreamily.

"What did you take?" Cammie demanded. They reached her car, and Adam leaned Mia against the hood.

"A couple of beers and a joint—what's the biggie?" Mia asked.

"No E? You didn't shoot or snort anything? You sure?"

"I don't do that stuff," Mia mumbled. "God, make a scene, why don't you? Hey, where's Dee?"

"Forget Dee," Cammie snapped. "We're going home."

Cammie opened the door, and Adam hoisted Mia into the backseat. Not only did Mia stop protesting as soon as she was horizontal, she fell asleep even before Cammie was out of the parking lot. Cammie fumed over Dee for a full five minutes before she explained to Adam exactly who Mia was.

"Wild child, huh?" Adam peered back at the snoring girl. "She looks about ten right now."

"Wild valley girl, the worst kind. God, what if we hadn't shown up?" Cammie asked.

She could feel Adam studying her in the dark. "You really care about her, huh?"

"No. I don't even like her."

"Then . . . ?" There was a question in his voice.

How could she explain? Cammie was hardly the type of girl to go around saving people from themselves. "I'm not getting all maudlin here, but after my mom died, I . . . I had some problems," she began. "My mom was really . . . She was great." Cammie swallowed the lump that welled up in her throat. She wasn't about to start crying, that was for sure. "By the time I was in middle school, I thought I was hot shit and all grown up. I looked for attention in a lot of really stupid, fucked-up ways. I'm lucky I lived through a lot of it."

"And?" Adam urged.

"And . . . I wish I'd had a big sister to save me from doing some of the stupid shit I did," Cammie admitted. "But I didn't."

"So you're doing it for Mia," Adam concluded.

"A little," Cammie conceded. "But mostly I'm doing it for me. Believe me, that doesn't mean I like her."

Adam's fingers reached under Cammie's hair to gently massage the back of her neck. "There really is more to Cammie Sheppard than meets the eye," he said softly.

"Don't let it get around."

God, his hand felt so good. He was so gentle and

nice and kind. How could a boy so sweet be so hot? But he was. He really was.

"You can help me get her inside," Cammie said. "And then we can go to my room. My father and step-mother are in a whole other wing of the house."

"I don't think that's a really good idea." He stopped rubbing her neck.

No, Cammie thought. That can't be. I don't get turned down. He's just nervous. Or maybe he's . . . That's it. He's a virgin. That's so sweet, in a way.

"It's really okay, Adam. I've got a lock on my door. And I know you'll be nervous, which is why—"

"It's not that. . . . Well, maybe it is, partly. I like you, Cammie. I'd like to get to know you better. I just have to get over this thing with Anna before I can—"

"Anna?" The name exploded from Cammie's lips.

"I know we weren't together that long," Adam went on. "But I still have feelings for her. And that really wouldn't be fair to you. So let's just take it slow, okay?"

Cammie clutched the steering wheel. She had just bared her soul to a boy she wanted and he had turned her down because he was still hung up on Anna Percy.

"Okay," Cammie said.

What she meant was: *Okay. Anna Percy's going to ruin everything if I don't do something. And soon, too.*

Behind the Mansion

Anna awakened on Sunday morning to the sound of an exquisite melody being played on the downstairs piano. She smiled and stretched, then snuggled under her velvet-and-silk quilt. This time she didn't wonder from where the glorious music was coming. She was just content to listen as Django played. What a terrific time she'd had the night before; she found Danny was so much fun to be with. He'd invited her to the Malibu beach house of one of the producers that afternoon. But the invitation had been extended in a completely casual and friendly way. Beyond that single kiss the night before, Danny hadn't tried anything or intimated that he was looking for more.

From Anna's point of view, it was perfect. She wasn't looking for more, either.

She listened to Django play until her stomach rumbled. Then she rose, put on a silk robe, and padded downstairs. She smelled fresh-brewed coffee and strawberries. Django looked up from the piano and gave her his semi-serious salute.

"Greetings and salutations, Miss Anna," he drawled.

Okay, this guy is great-looking, Anna thought. The bleached spiky hair, the ancient Levi's—and yes, even the cowboy boots—somehow worked on him.

"I don't suppose you could arrange this kind of wake-up call every morning," she said. "What smells so good?"

He rose from the piano bench. "My granny's top secret recipe for Cajun strawberry waffles. I left out the cottonmouth snake venom, but it's pretty close to the real thing. You hungry?"

"Starved," Anna admitted.

The dining room table had been set for two, with a snowy linen cloth. The centerpiece was a single rose from the rear garden in the Ming vase that was usually on the side table in the entryway. Anna had never seen it used before.

"Miss Anna." Django pulled out a chair for her.

"Thank you, sir. But if you call me 'Miss Anna' one more time, you're going to find granny's waffles flung across the room."

"I'll try to keep that in mind," Django replied archly. He forked two strawberry waffles onto Anna's plate. "If that's not the best thing you've ever tasted, I'll run naked down Rodeo Drive."

"Gee, I'm tempted to say I hate them," Anna teased. She cut into one and put a bite in her mouth. "Oh my God. This is fantastic."

"Gotcha." He grinned and cut into his own waffles. "One thing my grandmother can do is cook."

"Where is she?" Anna asked, taking a sip of her coffee.

"Louisiana." He pronounced it "Lou-see-yan-ah."

"It's a big state."

"She's a big woman."

Anna ate another few bites before she spoke again. "You don't talk much about your family."

"You don't like to talk much about yours, either. So, you have fun last night?" he asked, deftly changing the subject.

"Yes, I did, actually. I went to an over-the-top party on the *Hermosa Beach* set," Anna explained, forking another waffle onto her plate.

Django's eyebrows lifted. "Am I supposed to know what that is?"

"A new TV show. I forgot that you don't watch TV."

"As I recall, neither do you," Django reminded her. "Ben have fun, too?"

"He went back to school. And . . ." Anna hesitated. "It's over. We're not together anymore."

"Well, aren't you the heartbreaker of Beverly Hills." He took a sip of black coffee. "I knew he wasn't right for you."

Anna laughed. "Oh, you did, did you? How about if it's my turn to change the subject? Who taught you piano?"

"My piano teacher."

"Seriously. I'd like to know," Anna pressed.

"Well, hell, if I'm so good at being an enigma, why change now?" he drawled.

Anna put down her fork. "You gave me a jazz tape. You play classical enough to concertize. But you're working for my dad and living in his guesthouse. It doesn't make sense."

Django fiddled with the last piece of waffle left on his plate. "Didn't you ever want to reinvent yourself?"

"That's what brought me to Los Angeles," Anna confessed.

"Well, that's what brought me here, too."

"How did you meet my father in the first place?"

Django rubbed the stubble on his jaw. "He made a few investments for me. Index funds, put options, that sort of thing."

Curiouser and curiouser. Anna knew her father only managed the funds of corporations or the super-wealthy. But if Django had that kind of money, why wouldn't he just get his own place? And why would he have to work?

"Does my father know your mysterious story?" Anna pressed.

"Some of it," Django admitted.

She folded her arms. "You're making me insane."

Django's eyes seemed to linger on her lips for a moment. "You're makin' me insane, too."

Did he mean . . . ? Or was that just her imagination working overtime? God, what was wrong with her? Ben had just gone back to school. Last night she'd kissed Danny. There'd been Adam in between. And here she was, wondering if Django wanted to kiss her. When had she turned into such a—

Anna stopped her own train of thought. She suddenly realized: this was so Cyn-esque. Anna had wanted to be more like her daring best friend back in New York; now it was actually happening. If Jane Percy knew anything of her younger daughter's newly wicked ways, she'd probably hire well-bred men in Saville Row suits to have her deprogrammed. Because this behavior was anything but *This Is How We Do Things* Big Book, East Coast WASP edition.

"What are you smilin' about?" Django asked.

"Nothing. What were you were playing when I came downstairs?"

"Dunno." He shrugged. "I haven't given it a name yet."

"You wrote it?"

He scratched behind one ear. "Last I heard."

"You are so talented. You should be out there letting people hear what you—" Anna halted midsentence. "Look. I just got a great idea. I'd like to take your demo to the music supervisor of *Hermosa Beach.* Maybe they could use it on the show."

"Nice thought," Django said. "But I don't need your connections."

"Yes, you do. Or you wouldn't be living in a guest-house."

Django pushed his chair back and began to clear the table. "Thanks for the offer. If I change my mind, I'll let you know."

"But—"

"No 'buts,' Miss Anna," Django said.

She gathered up the silverware and coffee cups and followed him into the kitchen. "Are you sure?"

He put his things into the dishwasher, and she followed suit. "Yep," he said. "I'm sure. So let's not talk about it again."

Anna and Danny walked into the opulent living room of Arnold and Illyse Pink's beachfront home, where a bartender was serving up pitchers of Sex on the Beach, or, for those in AA—a goodly percentage of the television industry—Virgins on the Beach. A Persian rug was centered over the bleached wood floor. There was a white Ascherberg grand piano in the corner and next to it a music stand that held Bach sheet music. And a magnificent cello. There were platters of food everywhere—ribs and chicken wings and pigs-without-blankets, a sure sign that the Pinks were both on Atkins.

Arnold Pink was one of the producers on *Hermosa Beach.* He also produced three or four other network series and because of that rarely ventured to the set. Arnold had been a TV success story for two decades, and with that success came every luxury that money could buy, including his wife, Illyse, a *Maxim* model twenty-five years his junior.

At the moment the *Maxim* model was clad in a baby blue crocheted bikini and chatting up two of the male *Hermosa Beach* writers, who were having a hard time keeping their tongues in their mouths.

Anna and Danny took their drinks (Danny's was Sex, Anna's was Virgin) out to the star-shaped pool behind the mansion. Beyond that was the beach and then the endless ocean. "This is lovely," she told him as they stood at the edge of the pool deck, sipping their drinks.

"Streisand two houses to the right, Spielberg two houses to the left. One minute I tell myself it's worth putting up with all the crap to live between them someday," Danny mused. "Then I wake up in the middle of the night feeling like a total sellout who's never going to write his novel. And then I think I write TV because I know the novel will be . . . average. It won't suck, but it won't be great. It'll be just good enough to get some nice rejection letters. And I'll watch two years of work go down the drain."

"You're being a little hard on yourself."

"You're right," Danny cheerfully decided. "Nothing worse than an overprivileged guy whining about his overprivilege, huh?"

"Oh, I can think of a few things," Anna teased. "Such as—"

She was cut off by the ringing of Danny's cell. "Excuse me," he said, and plucked it out of his pocket. "Hello? . . . Yeah . . . Yeah . . . Okay, I'll be right there."

Danny hung up. A dark cloud had settled over his features. "What's wrong?" Anna asked.

"That was Clark, master and commander, summoning me back to the set."

"Now? You can't even have lunch?"

"Like I said, I'm a slave to TV." Danny sighed. "He's pissed about something or other. Just be glad he didn't ask for you, too."

Clark Super

Cammie had slept until noon, when Dee called to invite her and Mia to lunch at the Polo Lounge. Cammie took the opportunity to ream out the largely unapologetic Dee for having brought Mia to the rave in east L.A. Then she'd agreed to go to lunch but decided to stick it further to Dee by ordering a slew of expensive things and then nibbling at a bagel.

Now they were indoors at the Polo Lounge, enjoying the famous Sunday lunch. Mia showed no wear or tear from the night before. She'd polished off a smoked salmon omelet and three glasses of fresh-squeezed orange juice before declaring that she wanted to look at the shops on the downstairs promenade.

As for Cammie, she'd relented and merely ordered poached eggs. As Mia departed, she sat, assessing the lunchtime crowd—the mayor of Los Angeles sat at a rear table with Governor Schwarzenegger and his wife. Meanwhile Dee prattled on about a guy from Pasadena she'd met at the rave, a guy "way cooler" than Stevie, the guitarist with Border Crossing. As for Stevie, he'd returned to Brooklyn without even a "Thanks for the memories."

Cammie barely listened—she had a lot on her mind. Mostly Adam and his declaration that he couldn't or wouldn't be with Cammie until he was over Anna. Fuck Anna Percy. Revenge was going to be sweet.

". . . So I hope you accept my apology," Dee concluded.

Cammie focused on Dee's saucer-sized eyes. "What?"

"I said I'm really, *really* sorry I brought Mia last night. I guess I didn't think it through."

"You're forgiven," Cammie told her, feeling empowered. "Don't do anything that stupid again."

Dee nodded solemnly. "Cross my heart. I'll apologize to Mia, too."

"Are you kidding? She had a good time. Something to talk about with her friends in Valley Village."

"Yeah," Dee agreed. She opened her pink Hello Kitty purse—Cammie would have considered the purse an ironic statement except that Dee had no concept of irony—and handed something to Cammie. "A present. For you."

Cammie stared at the red, knotted Kabbalah bracelet. Kabbalah—the study and practice of Jewish mysticism—was all the rage in Hollywood. Thoroughly gentile Dee was taking classes with Madonna and Britney and had evidently decided she was a spiritual sage.

"Thanks, Dee. That's extremely . . . thoughtful." Cammie stuck the bracelet into her purse. The waitress brought the check and Dee put down one of her many credit cards. She glanced at the entryway to the Polo Lounge. "Mia's been downstairs too long."

"Maybe her stomach's upset from last night," Dee suggested.

"To quote the worst line in the history of Hollywood, 'I have a bad feeling about this,'" Cammie said. "Be back."

She slid out of the booth, left the Polo Lounge, and went downstairs to the promenade. There was no sign of Mia in any of the shops. She checked the downstairs bathroom, too.

"Mia?"

Nothing. Cammie peered at shoes under the stall doors. What the hell was Mia wearing on her feet? Delman white leather ballet flats under stall one: no. Knockoff Steve Madden platforms and fat ankles in stall two: definitely not. Stall three was Jimmy Choo stilettos in at least a size twelve—an obvious transsexual. Stall four was empty.

Damn her. Cammie marched back upstairs to the Polo Lounge, where Dee had just signed the credit card slip. "No go," she reported to Dee. "Let's check outside."

There were the usual two valets at the hotel entrance. Cammie accosted the older of them as he was unloading Louis Vuitton luggage from the back of a black limo.

"Have you seen a teen girl out here? Skinny, maybe five-four, red hair, puffy lips?"

The valet thought for a moment. "Yeah, actually. She came out here about fifteen minutes ago. With some other kids. They went toward the upper parking lot." He pointed to the right. "Now, excuse me. I'm busy here."

"Come on," Cammie told Dee. The two of them started toward the upper parking lot, where no one except the valets usually went. But they hadn't walked for more than five minutes when they heard peals of laughter coming from inside a small toolshed. Cammie recognized the laugh—Mia. She strode to the entrance of the shed and pulled the door open. There, sitting in a circle, were four middle-school-age kids. One of them held a bong. The shed reeked of high-quality reefer.

"Hi. Want some?" said the boy, holding the bong out to Cammie. That simple remark was enough to start the kids laughing again.

"Mia, what do you think you're doing?" Cammie asked, appalled that Mia was using such bad judgment as to get stoned in a place where she could easily be busted.

"This your mom, Mia?" the boy with the bong asked. More laughter followed.

"Fine," Cammie snarled. "Our car's leaving in five minutes, Mia. You'll either be there or not."

With that, Cammie closed the door.

Let her ruin her life, she thought. No one died and appointed me Superman. I'm not even her real sister.

Around ten that evening Anna was just about to climb into the bathtub when she heard a knock on her bedroom door. "Miss Anna?" someone called.

The voice was female. Anna slipped on her robe, walked through the bedroom, and opened the door. Juanita, one of her father's housekeepers, was at the door. She wore her coat over her uniform, and her purse was over her arm.

"I am just leaving and a man is here to see you," Juanita explained. "Clark Super."

Clark Sheppard, Anna thought automatically. Why would Clark come to her house on a Sunday night?

Anna thanked Juanita and followed her downstairs. Clark stood in the foyer; Juanita slipped out behind him.

"I wasn't expecting you," Anna said, feeling awkward. Yes, he was prone to call at any hour of the day or night, but to show up at her house was crossing the line.

"Turn on the TV," he barked.

"I beg your pardon?"

"Turn on the fucking TV!" he thundered. Without waiting for Anna to follow his direction, he marched into the living room, searched for and found the remote, and powered up the TV himself.

"What are you doing?" Anna asked.

"That's funny, coming from you."

She had no idea what he was talking about. The big screen filled with an image of Lynda Larson, host of *Hollywood Tonight,* the same show that had interviewed Jackson Sharpe at the party the night before.

"Tonight an *HT* exclusive: the inside scoop on the scandals and secrets of Arnold Pink's newest show, *Hermosa Beach.*" Footage of Scott Stoddard, the actor playing Cruise, that had been taken at the previous night's party, filled the screen. "Scott Stoddard, who plays the hunky male lead Cruise on the soon-to-premiere show *Hermosa Beach,* apparently has a secret past. He has been linked to a white supremacist group, the Aryan Alliance, with major followings in both America and England. According to our source, Stoddard attended Aryan Alliance meetings in both Idaho and Liverpool over the last two years and was involved in weapons training at both conclaves.

"*Hollywood Tonight* was tipped off by an inside source," Lynda continued, "a disgruntled *Hermosa Beach* insider. We wonder how this disclosure will affect the show's premiere in ten days, and—"

Clark snapped off the power. "Well?"

"Well, that's horrible," Anna said, bewildered. "But you could have just called and asked me to tune in."

"Why would you need to? You're the insider."

"I'm *what?*"

"I got a call from a friend on *Hollywood Tonight,*" Clark continued. "He warned me that this was running and that it was you who leaked it."

Anna shook her head at the bizarre accusation. "Me? But that's not possible! I don't know anything about these people. How could I?"

Clark stabbed a finger at Anna. "You have fucked the wrong person, Anna Percy. You're fired. And you will never eat breakfast, lunch, or dinner in this town again."

As he stormed out the door, Anna stood with mouth agape. Had that really just happened? She had to call Danny. Maybe he could make some sense of the insanity. She hurried upstairs and punched his number into her cell. He answered on the third ring.

"Danny? It's Anna."

"I'm in a meeting," he said, voice low.

"Clark was just here and he—"

"Look, I can't talk to you. I'll lose my job. Clark says you're dead to us."

D-Minus List

"Danny?"

"I told you last night, Anna. Clark says you're dead to us. That's a direct quote. I'm really sorry."

Anna clutched her cell tighter and turned away from the prying eyes in the BHH cafeteria. It was the next day at school, and she was at lunch. Though she'd tried to reach Danny repeatedly during the morning, he hadn't answered the phone. Now he had answered but still refused to talk to her.

"Don't hang up," she said quickly. "I didn't do it. I didn't. You know me better than that."

"Here's the deal. I like you. But I can't take sides. Not against Clark."

Anna was hurt. Profoundly. "I'm sorry you feel that way."

"This is my livelihood, okay?" Danny went on. "I can't screw around here. Everyone knows we were hanging out."

Anna's voice went Jane Percy icy; no one could cut someone cold quite the way Anna's mother could. "Fine. I'm sorry I called. I won't bother you again."

"Anna—"

This time it was Anna's turn to hang up.

"What you did is the bomb, girl! Fuck 'em!"

Anna turned to see an alt girl in combat boots and black tights give her a monster thumbs-up. But she didn't acknowledge it, just stared down into the vanilla yogurt she'd purchased. She could feel the eyes and hear the whispers. She had no idea how the news mill of BHH worked as quickly as it did, but by the time she'd arrived that morning, everyone knew she was The Insider Who Had Fucked *Hermosa Beach.* Most kids thought she was a traitor. A few thought she was beyond cool. No one asked whether the report was true or not.

The upshot was that Anna, who a mere week before had ascended to the heights of the BHH A-list, was now demoted to the D-minus list.

"Hi."

Anna looked up nervously. But it was only Sam, who slid a tray of Jell-O cubes and iceberg lettuce onto the table and sat across from her.

"Dining in?" Anna asked. With the exception of her brief flirtation with Power Eating, Sam hardly ever ate on campus.

"Penance for a weekend of utter gluttony," Sam explained. "So, is it true?"

Anna managed a half smile. "You're the first person all day to ask me that."

Sam spooned some Jell-O into her mouth. "Meaning you didn't?"

"Of course not!"

"I didn't think so. But Clark Sheppard has a way of making instant enemies," Sam explained. "Still, it didn't seem like your style. You just would have quit."

"No need. I got fired."

Sam squeezed a lemon wedge onto the lettuce. "Do we care?"

"Well, let's see. I blew my Apex assignment and got fired by Margaret. Then Clark fired me for creating a scandal. One more and I set a world record."

"Hey, cheer up. You never know how these things play out. The publicity might be good for the show. Scott Stoddard might go on *Sixty Minutes* and make a contrite apology. You'll be hailed as a hero and get a development deal at UPN."

Anna laughed. "This is a strange town, Sam."

Sam's eyes slid over to a girl who was wearing her lace bra *over* her T-shirt. "Land of insanity and fashion victims," she proclaimed. "That's showbiz." She took a bite of lettuce and made a face. "God, I'd kill for a Mars bar. Maybe I should get my stomach stapled."

"That's ridiculous," Anna said.

Sam pushed the tray away from her. "So let me ask you this. If it wasn't you, then who?"

Anna shrugged and dropped her chin into her hands.

"There are other interns," Sam pressed. "Why is everyone so sure it's you?"

"Because that's what someone at *Hollywood Tonight* told Clark."

Sam shook her head. "Come on, Anna. Where's your killer instinct? Think like a Los Angeleno, not like a New Yorker. Who'd want to make you look really, really, really bad?"

Slowly the truth dawned on Anna, who'd been so horrified by her situation that she'd barely thought about who'd framed her.

"Cammie?" she ventured.

"Aren't you bright," Sam said.

Anna sat up straighter. No. That was insane. "She would stoop this low? This is her father's show! Why would she want to hurt it?"

Sam shook her hair back. "I know Cammie. The answer is: yes, she would."

"But you can't just accuse her," Anna began. "Unless you know for a fact—"

"We don't," Sam admitted. "But I can help you find out."

Anna leaned forward. "How?"

Before Sam could answer, Adam loped by their table, barely nodding in their direction.

"She's even playing games with Adam's head now," Sam went on, "and he's the nicest guy I know."

Anna looped some hair that had come loose from her ponytail behind one ear. "In some ways I'd like to just forget the whole thing. It's all so sordid."

"Spoken like a girl of breeding," Sam teased. "But breeding doesn't get you squat in this town. I say, first we figure out what happened. Then we give as good as you got."

Pink-and-White Birthday Cake

Happy birthday to me, Cammie thought, and took another sip from her champagne flute. So what if she'd had to throw the party for herself? It had turned out great. She'd decided to hold it at Antebellum Daddy, a new bar down the block from Star Shoes, which, in Cammie's opinion, was already post-hip. House of Blues was way too obvious. And these days The Viper Room was filled with high-school kids with fake IDs.

Onstage Jared Leto's band, Thirty Seconds to Mars, was jamming. Over at the bar kids Cammie knew vaguely from school were swigging this week's stupid drink trend from Pooh Bear baby bottles: cough syrup with codeine mixed with Hennessey. Cammie preferred to stick to Cristal champagne. She glanced at the dance floor and grinned. Not only had all her friends showed up, but a number of celebrities, too. Kirsten was dancing with Tobey, Dee was dancing with Adam, and Sam with Parker's younger brother, Monty.

Cammie had planned her affair carefully, right down

to the departure gift bags that each guest would take
away. The girls and women would each get a big assortment of Mario Badescu skin care products, a Levi's
Type 1 jean jacket, a Jacobson/Mann ancient coin neck-
lace, and a Kiko watch on the underside of whose
leather band had been etched *Cammie 18.* The guys
would each get the newest iPod, a sleeve of the new
Calloway golf balls, and the same Kiko watch as the
girls, except with a more masculine band.

Adam worked his way through the crowd, balancing
two plates of food from the buffet. He handed one to
Cammie. "Everyone over there is saying how great the
food is. You throw a hell of a party."

To Cammie, these words momentarily underscored
the sad fact that she'd had to organize her own affair, but
she grinned anyway. Those days were over: happy days
were here again, Anna Percy was hiding in her room, and
being with Adam just about made up for everything else.
Jared's band took the pace down a notch, and Cammie
indicated a nearby table. She put her plate down and
motioned for Adam to do the same. "We can eat later."

She led him to the dance floor, where they embraced
and he smiled down at her. "You look beautiful."

She already *knew* that. But it was sweet of him to say
so. "So do you."

They danced a few beats in silence. "About the other
night," he began. "What I said about Anna—"

"I'd prefer not to discuss her at *my* birthday party, if
you don't mind."

"Fair enough," he agreed.

"She treated you like shit, Adam," she went on, despite her own edict. "I mean, think about it. What does it say about you if you're hung up on a girl who does that?"

"I'm not 'hung up' on her, exactly. I'm not very good at bouncing from relationship to relationship."

"I understand," Cammie sympathized, though she thought Adam was slightly full of shit. *Relationship?* He and Anna had been together for a nanosecond in between Anna's pathetic Ben Birnbaum binges.

"You see, Cammie—"

"Shhh." She raised her lips to Adam's and kissed him softly. Once again electricity surged through her. Adam was hot in a completely different way from Ben. But hot he definitely was.

When the band took a break, Sam made her way over to Cammie. "Great party."

"Yuh. Thanks for all your help with it," Cammie said, dripping sarcasm.

"I've been really busy lately."

"I could tell. With your NBF Anna Percy," Cammie commented, using the derisive Hollywood term for "new best friend." It was always used pejoratively, on the assumption that your NBF today would become a PYOK (person you once knew) tomorrow.

Sam shook her hair out of her eyes. "What happened to her sucks. She was framed."

Cammie folded her arms, secure in the knowledge

that one of the smartest decisions she'd ever made was never to poke around in her father's office. All these years the temptation had been great—who could imagine what she might find in his file drawers and on his computer?—but she'd always resisted.

So when she finally opened the door and hunted around for something she could use to screw Anna, she was sure that no one would suspect. It hadn't taken long for her to find the manila folder in his "actors" file that held a background check on Scott Stoddard . . . and the damning information about his sickening political affiliations. A quick phone call to *Hollywood Tonight* had closed the deal. Score: Cammie one, Anna zero.

"And I would care because—?" Cammie asked lightly.

"No reason," Sam replied. "But I *am* going to figure out who did it."

"Now that the two of you are such great friends?"

Sam held Cammie's gaze. "We *are* friends, Cammie. Just like I'd like us to be friends."

"Well, that's so sweet," Cammie said with a smile. "Little Miss Anna may have you fooled, Sam, but you're as gullible as Dee, only with thirty more IQ points."

Sam shook her head. "You can't play me—"

"Who's playing you? Wake up and smell the coffee. She may look like an ice queen, but Anna is a user. She'll use you just like she used Ben, and Adam, and God knows how many other people. Who knows why she came here? Maybe she was run out of her school in New York for that!"

Cammie saw the flash of insecurity in Sam's eyes and felt a glimmer of triumph. But when Sam baby-stepped away, she felt something else, too. Sadness. Sam was the closest thing Cammie had to a real best friend—a friendship that had stood the test of time. That connection was one more thing Anna Percy had robbed from her.

"Happy birthday to you, happy birthday to you . . ."

The lights dimmed; Cammie turned and saw a big group of her friends wheeling out her four-tiered, pink-and-white birthday cake. The whole club joined in on the song, with Jared's band providing impromptu backing. The cart with the cake stopped in the middle of the dance floor—Cammie strode over to it and blew out her candles with one impressive gust of air. When she did, the room burst into cheers and applause. Then pink-and-white balloons dropped from ceiling nets, tumbling over the guests like at a political convention.

It was a hell of a party, even though it was a week-night. At two in the morning Cammie held court at a table of fifteen of her closest friends. As unobtrusively as possible, Antebellum Daddy's special events coordinator—a young woman named Jennifer—approached, holding a European-style portable credit card machine.

"Want some champagne?" Cammie asked, grabbing a bottle by the neck and lifting it in Jennifer's direction.

The young woman smiled. "Maybe in a bit. But we have a minor problem. Your credit card was declined."

Cammie laughed loudly. "That's ridiculous. You

authorized it when we planned this affair. Just try it again."

"I did. Three times. Do you have another card? These things happen sometimes."

Cammie frowned, opened her Prada purse, and dug out another credit card.

Declined. The table hushed as people figured out what was going on, all eyes on Cammie.

"Must be something in the air!" Cammie joked, finding another one and handing it to the events planner. Declined. And another. Declined. Cammie felt sick to her stomach. She'd run through all her major credit cards. It wouldn't do much good to give Jennifer her gift card for Starbucks.

Adam slid into the empty seat next to Cammie, holding another big piece of birthday cake. He saw the concern on Cammie's face. "Is there a problem?"

"No, of course not," Cammie said. She stared down Jennifer. "Look, Jenni-poo, there is obviously something wrong with your machine."

"Nope. In the back office I called Visa and MasterCard and American Express before I came out here. Everything's fine."

"Of all the—" Cammie whirled to Adam and held out her hand. "Lend me your Visa?"

Adam shrugged. "Don't have one."

The table broke up in laughter, both at Cammie's discomfiture and the idea that one of their peers would live in Los Angeles without a credit card.

Cammie saw Dee across the table. "Dee! I need your Visa."

"What for?" Dee asked sassily. Again people laughed, since it was perfectly obvious why.

Cammie glared at her impertinence. "Come on. I need it."

Dee shrugged, fished into the back pocket of her low-slung velvet pants, and pushed her Visa card across the table, where Cammie slapped it into Jennifer's hand. "When that card doesn't go through, you owe me one big, fat apology."

Jennifer looked at Dee. "The tab is over ten thousand dollars—"

"Do I need to speak more slowly or what?" Cammie interrupted. "She's not *paying*. If mine is declined, hers is declined. Just put it through."

Jennifer shrugged and ran Dee's card through the machine. Within seconds a receipt for Dee spat out of the machine.

"Uh, Cammie?" Dee ventured as an even bigger crowd of onlookers gathered around the table, whispering and pointing at Cammie.

"Shit!" Cammie tore up the receipt and let it fall to the floor. Then she got an idea. "Cancel that transaction, please. And do you accept this?" It was her bank debit card. Last she checked there was enough money in her account to feed a small nation for a year.

"Sure. Run it yourself," Jennifer said, holding out the machine for her.

Cammie did. DECLINED flashed on the little screen.

"I'd talk with my financial adviser if I were you," Jennifer quipped, to a roar of laughter from the crowd.

"Did you cancel my friend's transaction?" Cammie whispered, feeling defeated.

"No."

"Good." Cammie held the Visa receipt out to Dee. "Sign this."

Dee flinched. "It's a *loan*, right?"

"No, Dee, I think you should pay for this fucking party as my birthday present. Of course it's a loan. I'll write you a check as soon as I get home."

Jennifer found a pen, Dee signed her name, and the transaction was quickly completed. The spectacle over, the crowd broke up, everyone sure they had a hell of a story to report the next day to anyone unlucky enough not to have been there.

Yet the story wasn't over. A half hour later Adam had his arm around her as they left the club and walked to her car—her birthday presents would be delivered by the club the next day. Cammie had partially rallied: Adam didn't seem too fazed by what had happened and even made some kind remark about the intricacies of the electronic banking system. To Cammie's credit, she hadn't made the mistake of asking him to come home with her. She knew her best strategy was to play it cool: good things come to those who wait.

But as they approached the club's private parking

structure, she saw a tow truck pull out. It had a BMW on its flatbed.

"Hey!" Cammie said, recognizing the vehicle. "That's my car. Stop!"

She ran over to the tow truck with Adam and banged on the window. "What the hell are you doing?" She kept banging on the window until the driver rolled down the glass.

"Sorry, miss, nothing I can do," the driver said.

"Well, it's a mistake!" Cammie yelled. *"That's my fucking car!"*

The tow truck started rolling again. Cammie stood, dumbfounded, as her BMW disappeared into the night.

Dee ending up driving Cammie home, dropping Adam on the way. As she drove, Cammie tried to make light of the bizarre end to her party, claiming that it had to be some strange misunderstanding.

"Thanks for the help, Dee," Cammie said as Dee pulled up in front of her home. "I mean it."

"No need to thank me," Dee chirped. "But write me a check tomorrow."

"Night." She turned and headed inside. There sat her father, stepmother, and Mia in the living room, one cozy little family.

"What a weird night. What's everyone doing up?" Cammie asked.

"Waiting for you," Patrice said, her voice dripping icicles.

"But it's after midnight, Patrice," Cammie pointed out. "Don't you turn back into a witch and go riding off on your broom?"

"See how mean she is?" Mia asked. "She's always this mean!"

"I'm not in the mood for a late night soiree, okay?" Cammie asked rhetorically. "I had the most hellacious experience. My credit cards got declined and my bank debit card, and then my Beemer—"

"Got towed," her father finished for her. He was sitting like a king on the Louis XVI chair at the far end of the living room.

Cammie trudged to the couch and slumped onto it. "How did you know?"

"Because I had it towed," her father said.

Cammie sat up. She looked from her father, to her stepmother, to Mia. Mother and daughter shared a smug countenance. But her father looked like a storm cloud about to burst.

"What the hell is going on?" Cammie demanded.

Her father stood and put his hands on his hips. "Of all the self-centered, bitchy, thoughtless things you've ever done, Camilla, this takes the damn cake."

Camilla? He *never* called her Camilla.

"What are you talking about?"

"You fucked with my TV show." His voice was low but filled with fury. "My show!"

Cammie tried hard to keep her cool. "I did not."

"Yes, you did," Mia piped up. "I heard you call

Hollywood Tonight from Dad's home office. And you said you were that girl, Anna."

"And I say you're a pathological little liar," Cammie seethed.

Mia shook her head. "Anna and Sam Sharpe said they needed to talk to me. They took me out to dinner. They told me how they thought you hurt Anna even though she never did anything mean to you. It made me think about how mean you are to me all the time. So I told them the truth."

Cammie could feel a lump rise in her throat. She was just so tired, tired of everything and everyone. "Fine, I did it," she jeered as she got to her feet. "You should be proud, Dad. I learned about playing dirty from you."

Her father looked disgusted. "No, you didn't. No one cares about this Anna. But you fucked with my TV show over some stupid teenage vendetta. I don't care about your vendetta. *But you don't shit where you live,* Camilla. You haven't learned anything!"

"But I wasn't trying to hurt you, Dad—"

He raised a hand to silence her. "Save it. Right now you have no credit cards, no bank account, and no car. If I get any madder, I'll give your clothes away and you can shop at Costco." He put a finger in his daughter's face. "Don't you ever, *ever* fuck with me again. Do you hear me?"

Cammie managed to hold her head high. "I hear you. Now you hear me. It's my birthday. My eighteenth birthday. I'm the only child you have—even if the brat over there does call you 'Dad.' You don't care about me. All you care about is your office, your work, your show. So if you want to be ashamed of someone, look in the mirror."

Then she turned and walked to the stairs so she could cry in her room in peace.

Stand in Line

"Miles loves me. I'm having Miles's baby!" the actress cried.

"Wake up, Belinda. Miles only loves himself!" the actress playing her mother insisted.

God, soap operas were awful, Cammie thought as she flipped through the channels of the big-screen TV in her bedroom.

Though it was past noon, Cammie still wore nothing more than the underwear in which she'd fallen asleep. She'd brushed her teeth because she detested morning mouth, but there wasn't really any point in dressing. There was no way she was going to school. She couldn't even muster the energy to see if her father had reinstated her credit cards or her bank account or brought her car home.

She picked up the framed photo of her mother that she kept on her nightstand. Then she looked at her wall and its half-completed mural of the characters from *Charlotte's Web*. She and her mother had been working on that mural when her mom had died all those years ago. When Clark had purchased this home, Cammie had insisted that the mural move with the rest of her stuff. Yet it would always be half finished, a reminder of Cammie's loss.

There was a knock on her door. "Go away," she barked.

"A boy is here to see you," one of the housekeepers called.

"Who?" Cammie called back.

"Go find out."

Fine. Great. Just what she needed—a surly attitude from the domestic help. Cammie pulled on the first thing she found: an old tennis warm-up jacket and some drawstring pajama bottoms. Then, still barefoot, she went downstairs.

Adam stood in the front hallway. He was carrying a bunch of white daisies.

"Hi," he said. He thrust the daisies at her. "These are for you."

Daisies. Cammie had always thought of them as flowering weeds that the gardeners were forever pruning out of the garden. Daisies looked ordinary and smelled foul. You gave daisies to ten-year-old girls in Idaho, not to Cammie Sheppard. But these daisies were magnificent.

"You weren't at school this morning," Adam went on. "It was a rough night. I came to see if you're okay."

"You don't have a car. How'd you get here?"

"Bike," Adam sheepishly admitted. "Don't let it get around."

"That's three miles. Uphill!"

Adam shrugged. "Strong legs."

"That was really nice of you," Cammie said. And she meant it, too. She asked him to come into the kitchen with her so that she could find a vase and water. Her reflection in the stainless steel refrigerator reminded her that she looked a wreck: unwashed, unbrushed, un–made up. "I look like hell."

"Actually, I like it," Adam mused as Cammie arranged the flowers in a handblown Belgian glass vase. "I don't think I've ever seen your real face before."

Now he revealed something from behind his back that Cammie hadn't even realized he was carrying.

It was a small, wrapped gift.

"I didn't want to give this to you last night with all those other gifts," he confessed. "Prada and Yada and Whadda and I don't know what all." He scratched the star tattoo behind his ear. "Anyway . . ."

He handed her the package. She tore the wrapping open. It was a first edition of *Charlotte's Web.* "Look at the title page," he suggested.

She leafed to the title page. It was signed by the author, E. B. White. Cammie had done a report on E. B. White when she was in sixth grade. She knew how the author hated to autograph his own books. Where had Adam found this one?

"I remember you mentioned once that *Charlotte's Web* made you think of your mom," Adam explained. "So I found this on eBay."

Cammie pursed her lips. "This is the best gift any-one ever gave me." She put the book on the gleaming butcher-block counter, went to Adam, and embraced him. "Thank you." She started to kiss him but changed her mind. Instead she put her head on his shoulder. He stroked her hair like he would a child's.

"You're welcome. I guess I should go," he said finally.

"Wait. Do you really have to go back to school? I mean, could you . . . would you . . . ?" She gulped hard as she stepped away from him and gazed into his wel-coming eyes. "I'd really like to be with you right now. We could go to . . . to the park by the elementary school. To the swings. Anything."

Oh God. Had she just said that? How pathetically vulnerable and needy did she sound? What if he turned her down? Of course he was going to turn her down; he was Mr. Straight Shooter and he was going to get on his little bike and pedal back to—

"Let's do it," Adam said.

Cammie's eyes lit up. "Really?"

He laughed. "You look about six years old. Yeah, really. My GPA can take it."

"I don't even know if there's a car I can take—" Cammie began.

"We can walk."

"Walk . . . right!" It seemed like an adventure to Cammie, who never walked anywhere. "I'll go get dressed. Wait right here."

She ran upstairs, giddy with happiness. She was going to spend the afternoon in the park with Adam. He was so straight. And honest. And nice. He was probably a virgin, for godsake.

But go figure: Cammie Sheppard was losing her heart to him anyway.

". . . So you can have your job back," Clark concluded.

He'd called Anna at school to inform her that he was rehiring her since he'd determined she hadn't been the culprit with *Hollywood Tonight.* There'd been no apology, just an order to be on the set right after school.

It was a beautiful day, so Anna was outside in the courtyard, eating lunch with Sam at the same picnic table where the newspaper editor had accosted her about doing an interview for the school paper. "Mr. Sheppard, if I were dirt poor and you were paying me in diamonds, I wouldn't take back the internship," Anna told him. "There is no excuse for the way you treated me."

"It's Clark?" Sam asked, raising her eyebrows. "Tell him to go to hell!"

Anna smiled and shushed her as Clark replied. "Hey, that's showbiz. If you're going to be that touchy, you'll never get anywhere in this town."

"Well, then, that works very neatly with my plans. Thank you and have a pleasant life." Anna disconnected him. It gave her a great deal of satisfaction to do it.

"Nice," Sam said. "Now you can concentrate on our screenplay."

"True."

"You want to go to Bev's after school and throw some ideas around?"

Anna shook her head. "Actually, I have to go to the set after school. *Hermosa Beach.*"

"Uh, hello—Anna doesn't work there anymore."

"I know," Anna replied. "But Anna definitely has some unfinished business there. How about dinner?"

"Sounds good," Sam agreed. "Call me later and we'll pick a place."

"Did you ever eat Ethiopian?" Anna asked.

Sam grinned. "No. And I'm not starting now." She got up and headed back toward the main building.

But Anna called to her. "Sam!"

Sam turned and took a couple of steps back toward Anna.

"Thanks," Anna said. "For believing me. For helping me talk to Mia. For going against Cammie. She's going to hate you now. And . . . well, everything."

A smile lit up Sam's face. "I'm sure you'd do the same for me."

And so I would, Anna thought. And so I would.

By the time Anna reached the *Hermosa Beach* set, it was nearly four o'clock. No one paid much attention to her; one intern more or less wasn't exactly news on the set of a TV show about to premiere. She found Danny in his office, typing into his computer. She sat uninvited on his couch. "Hello."

"Interesting opening line," Danny mused. "Is it followed by, 'I hate your guts'?"

"No," Anna said. "You were right. You didn't have any reason to believe me or to risk your job over it."

Danny swiveled his chair around to face her. "Well, for what it's worth, I'm sorry."

"Were you planning to tell me that?" Anna asked.

"No," he confessed. "I'd already moved on to the 'she hates your guts' thing. I figured you'd never want to hear from me again."

"I've decided to let you make it up to me."

He laughed. "Oh, really?"

"Yes, really," she teased. "You can take me out and lavish me with attention and excellent jokes. In return, I may forgive you. When can I pencil you in?"

"Now."

Anna was taken aback. "Now? But you never leave the office in the middle of the—"

Danny jumped up from his desk, took her hand, and pulled her out of his office and down the hall. They stopped outside the door of the script supervisor. "Hey, Jimbo. If anyone asks, tell 'em I'm out for a couple of hours."

"You can't leave," the script supervisor retorted. "Clark's around. What if he needs you?"

"Tell him it was an emergency!" He turned to Anna. "This calls for a fast getaway."

They hightailed it down the hall, out the ocean-side doors of the hotel and toward the ocean. Danny quickened his pace until he was fairly flying across the sand. Anna followed, breathless with laughter.

"You're insane!" Anna cried as Danny whirled, picked her up, and then tumbled together with her to the sand. "The sun will be down in a minute. We'll freeze out here."

"That is then, this is now." Danny propped himself up on his elbows and looked out at the ocean. "What do you see, Anna?"

She thought a moment. "Possibilities."

"Me too." He leaned over and kissed her lightly. "Could you like a writer who's less than five-foot eight and went to a public university and may never write the great American novel?"

"Maybe you will. Or . . ." She paused and grinned at him. "Maybe I'll write it first."

"Touché, Anna Percy. But you didn't answer the other part."

"Why do you think I'm here?"

His answer was to kiss her again. The first guy Anna had ever loved was Scott Spencer. But Scott had fallen for her best friend Cyn and never seemed to know that Anna existed. The second boy she had loved was Ben. But that had become so intense, so fast, that she couldn't separate the getting to know him from the lust of wanting him.

And now there was Danny. She wasn't sure what they would be or even *if* they'd be. But she liked him, and he wasn't likely to get all heavy with her or try to rush her into something for which she wasn't ready. Because there were other boys—Django . . . and even Adam—that she thought about. Maybe lots of other boys. Maybe lots of boys she hadn't even met yet.

Maybe she was going to be so busy writing a movie with Sam that all the boys would just have to stand in line.

Anything was possible. Anything.

The only thing harder than
getting in is staying in.

THE CLIQUE

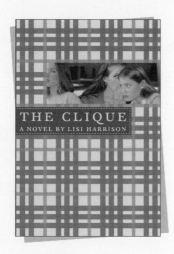 

Be sure to read both novels in the juicy
CLIQUE series, and keep your eye out for REVENGE
OF THE WANNABES, coming May 2005.